SOLID GROUND

WENDY SMITH

Photography and Cover Design by
GOLDEN CZERMAK / FURIOUSFOTOG

Model
SEAN RAE

All rights reserved. No part of this book may be reproduced or transmitted in any form, including electronic or mechanical, without written permission from the publisher, except in the case of brief quotations embodied in critical articles or reviews.

This is a work of fiction. Names, characters, businesses, places, events, and incidents are either the products of the author's imagination or used in a fictitious manner. Any resemblance to actual persons, living or dead, or actual events is purely coincidental. Wendy Smith is in no way affiliated with any brands, songs, musicians or artists mentioned in this book.

© Wendy Smith 2024

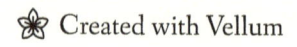

❦ Created with Vellum

ONE
DECLAN

LAS VEGAS.

Sin City.

The city that never sleeps.

Always my favourite place to lose myself after finishing a film.

And honestly? The crappy, destined-to-go-straight-to-DVD film I just made will probably be my last.

My career is over.

It's a sobering thought. And I'll get sober just as soon as I have one last weekend of debauchery.

For about the millionth time, my mobile rings and I silence the call. My agent, Nikki, has been hounding me since my film wrapped. No doubt she's got other shitty offers on the table.

For almost thirty years I've ridden the roller coaster that is Hollywood. I've lived the highs, both figurative and literal, and now I've sunk into this bottomless pit of despair.

I'm not making another never-will-be-seen movie ever again.

Maybe I'm not the type to retire to the country and live a quiet life, but something has to be better than my dying career. I need a break—some alone time to come to grips with who I am. My life has been a whirlwind since my teens.

Now I'm in my mid-forties and I want to take some time to breathe.

I've been working since I was a teenager—my "big break" came in the form of a soap opera, and while I've been blessed to be a jobbing actor since, it hasn't all been smooth sailing.

It's my own fault for driving my career into the ground. The alcohol and the partying pushed people too far. There are directors and other actors who refuse to work with me because of mistakes I've made along the way.

I'm getting off this ride before I truly hit rock bottom.

I'm in the hotel lobby when my mobile rings again, and I groan before hitting accept.

I might as well get this over with.

"Nikki."

"I've got an offer—"

"Answer's no."

She sighs. "But this could be the step back to—"

"That's what you said last time. And the time before." I growl. "I'm done. It's over. I'm going to live it up this weekend and then go home to LA to hide behind the giant metal fences I've surrounded my house with."

"And do what? You'll climb the walls with nothing to do."

I let out a sigh. "No idea yet. Become a farmer? Grow corn? I don't know, but something has to be better than this."

She huffs. "Fine. Take a break. But you know that there's more for you out there. We just need to get you back on track."

"I'm not sure I want to 'get back on track'."

There's a pause on the other end of the line. "You're serious, aren't you?"

"I am. I've had it with this life."

"Okay. Okay." She draws a deep breath. "I'll back off. Have fun this weekend, and we'll talk again next week. I don't want to give up on you, Declan. I don't think you should give up on you either."

"Thanks, Nikki. Love you." I hang up before she can respond with the snort I usually get back when I profess my feelings for her. She's been a part of my life for so long, she's practically family, but I'm not caving on this.

My career is well and truly over.

I thought I'd be more upset than I am, but it's time. My only regret is that I didn't retire several years ago before the flops and the direct-to-DVD movies.

I'm already checked into the Bellagio, so I head downstairs to find a bar and a drink.

There was a time in my career when going out in public was hard. Being recognised was a pain in the ass, and there were occasions when I needed security with me.

I'm not sure I miss those days.

While I'm still recognised on a regular basis, there are no security concerns. Sometimes I'll be stopped for a selfie or an autograph, but those times are few and far between.

It's just as well because I'm rarely in the right frame of mind to deal with requests.

By the time I've had a couple of drinks, I'm warmed up and ready to look for a good time. I'm not out to get laid—if I drink as much as I plan to, I doubt I'd be able to perform. I want to party and have fun.

I turn around and lean back on the bar, scanning the dance floor.

It's her swaying hips that catch my eye at first.

I've always preferred brunettes.

And this one is spectacular.

Her little black dress hugs her curves, her long dark hair swinging as she waves her arms in the air and dances with a shorter blonde.

The blonde's not bad-looking either, but it's the brunette that grabs my attention like no one else in that room.

The look of sheer joy on her face draws me to her. Her smile is a mile wide, her eyes sparkling as she laughs with her friend.

The blonde stumbles, and concern crosses the brunette's face as she catches her and guides her to a nearby booth.

Before I know it, I'm on my feet and making my way toward them.

"Hey," I call out.

They don't hear me, the brunette brushing the hair from the blonde's face, her brow furrowed in concern.

I step closer. "Hey. Is she okay?"

The brunette's blue-eyed gaze hits me, and I almost take a step back. From afar, she was gorgeous, but up close—she's spectacular. Even in the dim lighting of the bar, the freckles smattered across her button nose are visible.

Her full lips twitch as she fixes those beautiful eyes on me. "Um I thought she was, but I think she's had too much to drink. We'll be fine. Thanks for checking on us."

That's not an American accent, but with the music playing, it's hard to hear what it is.

"Do you need a hand?"

She shrugs. "As long as I can get her back to our room, we should be okay."

"Are you sure I can't help?"

Chewing her bottom lip a moment, she hesitates.

I hold up my palms. "If you want, I can call the bar staff. I'm sure they've dealt with this kind of thing before."

She glances at her friend. "I don't really want to make a scene. Caitlin's fiancé is kind of famous and ..."

"It's okay. You're staying at the Bellagio?"

She nods.

"Let's get her out of here."

Caitlin looks up. "Ohh I know you who are." Caitlin giggles and points. "Zoe, it's Declan O'Leary."

I grin. "Good spotting."

"My mom loves you."

Zoe snorts, and I shift my gaze to her, raising an eyebrow.

"I'm sorry for my friend. She's so good at putting her foot in her mouth. Especially when she's wasted."

I shrug. "It's fine. We all have bad nights. I've had a few myself." Shifting my gaze to Caitlin, I tilt my head. "Can you walk?"

In response, I get another peal of laughter, and Zoe rolls her eyes.

"Come on, you," she says.

I lean down. "Wrap your arm around my shoulders, sweetheart. I'll help you."

"I can't believe Declan O'Leary is helping me to my room." She giggles again and Zoe and I help her to her feet.

"I've got her," I say to Zoe, but as we leave the bar and approach the elevators, it becomes increasingly obvious that I don't have her. Her legs buckle out from underneath her, and it takes a lot of extra effort to hold her up.

Zoe presses the button and a door opens. After stepping into the elevator, I sweep Caitlin up into my arms. At least she won't stumble now.

The elevator starts to move.

"Thank you so much for this," Zoe says. "I doubt she'll remember much in the morning. So much for our first trip to Vegas."

"How did she get so drunk? The bars are usually more careful."

Zoe shrugs. "Too much too fast. I was pacing myself because we're here for two nights, but she had other ideas. She's also not very good at handling her booze."

Now we're in the quiet, I can hear Zoe better. Her accent's definitely not American. I've worked with Australians before, and it's not that. Maybe New Zealand?

"You're not from around here."

She grins. "What gave it away?"

"Well…"

The elevator dings and the doors slide open. I follow Zoe down the hallway until we come to a stop outside a room.

It's much smaller than my own, and there are two matching queen-size beds. Zoe points me toward the one closest to the windows.

As I dip to place Caitlin on the mattress, she falls face-first and laughs. I turn to leave, and by the time I've reached the door, a loud snore comes from the other side of the room.

Zoe and I share a bemused glance.

"So much for partying the night away," Zoe says.

"Was that the plan?"

Zoe nods. "Caitlin's getting married in two weeks. Neither of us have ever been to Las Vegas. We thought we'd run away for the weekend to celebrate."

"And now she's out for the count and it's still early." I chuckle.

She blows out a long breath. "Yep. This wasn't how I saw tonight going."

For a moment, I study her. "I've got a proposition for you."

Zoe's eyebrows shoot up, and she runs her tongue along that scarlet top lip. "You do?"

"Your friend is out for the count, and this is your first time in Vegas. Let's not waste your night."

Her smile is warm, and I know I've hit the target.

"What do you suggest?"

"Leave her a note in case she wakes up. We'll add my number to it so she's got contact details for both of us. I'll show you around, and then we can come back here and drink the complimentary champagne in my penthouse suite."

Her face lights up in a grin, and her blue eyes sparkle.

"That sounds like a great plan." She hesitates, her gaze returning to the bed.

"We can come back here and check on her after our tour and before we go up to my suite. You said she hadn't had a lot to drink."

Zoe nods. "It doesn't take much to get her drunk. A couple of glasses of wine do it sometimes. She's crashed on my couch before."

"If you'd rather not go, that's okay too. I won't hold it against you." I wink at her, and her cheeks flush pink.

She watches Caitlin for a moment. "No. I still want to see Las Vegas before we leave. I don't know if I'll make it back here for another visit before the end of the year."

"What's happening at the end of the year?"

Zoe's gaze swings back to me. "I finish my current contract and then depending on what happens, I might be going back to New Zealand."

I smile. "We don't have to be gone long. Even if it's an hour or so." I take her hands in mine. "But if you want to take a rain check, that's all good too."

"A rain check?"

"We do this another time when your friend isn't drunk."

Her blue eyes sparkle. "You would do that?"

"I really want to spend some time with you. Maybe we can swap numbers. Plan our own clandestine Las Vegas adventure." I grin. I'm not sure what it is about this woman, but I want to spend time with her. "Let's swap numbers and we'll sort this out later."

She nods and gives me her number. I type it in and send her a quick text.

"It was nice meeting you, Zoe. Shame about the circumstances, but that can't be helped."

Zoe laughs. "Thank you for all your help, Declan. I'd never have been able to get her back to the room without it."

"You're welcome."

TWO
ZOE

I LIE on my bed and look up at the ceiling. Declan left an hour ago, and I'm still debating whether I should have taken him up on his offer or not.

Caitlin still lets out the odd snore, but she's clearly okay. I should have made her eat something before we went down to the bar, but she was in such a rush to start our weekend that I didn't push it.

Though if she hadn't been so drunk I might not have met Declan.

He's gorgeous. I've seen him in movies before, but never thought I'd get to see him up close and personal. And now I have his phone number.

"Zoe? Why am I in bed?" Caitlin slurs.

"Because you had three glasses of wine and couldn't walk properly."

She laughs. "I'm such a lightweight."

"Yes, yes you are."

"Did I dream that Declan O'Leary carried me to our room?"

I bite my bottom lip and smile to myself. "No, that was real."

"What?"

"He offered me a driving tour of Las Vegas."

Her blonde head pops up. "So why are you here?"

"I couldn't really abandon you when you're unconscious."

She shrugs. "I'm fine."

"I've got his number. He said we could have a rain check."

Caitlin flops back down. "So, call him. What's the time?"

I sigh. "A little after ten."

"Call him now. Tell him you want to go tonight. I'm going back to sleep."

"Are you sure?" I glance at my phone.

"Yes. Go. How many times in your life do you think you're going to get the chance to hang out with a movie star like Declan O'Leary?" She sounds so tired. I don't know if it's just the alcohol—she's been labouring over this wedding for months.

"Only if you're sure …"

"I'll push you out the door," she mumbles. "Go and have fun."

Picking up my phone, I take a deep breath and start a text.

Me: *It's Zoe. Caitlin is okay and insisting I go out. Still want to show me around?*

It only takes a moment for him to reply.

Declan: *I'd love to. I'll call my driver. Meet you in the lobby in ten minutes.*

I'm not sure what I'm doing.

I don't know this guy, but I'm about to get in a car and tour Las Vegas with him.

This was supposed to be mine and Caitlin's weekend together. In two weeks she's getting married to Brandon, her NFL-player boyfriend. He's just been transferred to a team in Chicago, so soon after the wedding, my best friend will move more than three thousand kilometres away.

I only have a year left on my current contract, and before then I'll need to work out what my next move is and whether I can stay on in the US versus going home to New Zealand.

It feels like I'll be losing all the good things in my life in the next few months.

So to hell with being good. I've lived my whole life as the good girl, the one who never rebelled, who never did anything crazy.

And I think spending the evening with Declan could be classified as that.

I make my way down to the lobby. It's impossible to miss him. He's tall—over six feet, and that star presence rolls off him in waves. He's a blinding light in a sparkling city.

Maybe it's the smile that graces his lips as I approach, or the utter delight in his eyes as he catches my gaze, but that star power is turned on me.

My heart beats faster.

"I didn't think I'd hear from you quite so soon," he says.

I shrug. "I didn't expect Caitlin to wake up. She's gone

back to sleep, but before she did, she told me to go out and enjoy myself."

His grin is addictive. I'm sure this man has been with some of the world's most beautiful women, but right now he wants to spend time with me.

"I'm glad you changed your mind. Are you ready to go?"

"If you are."

He's a Hollywood star who's older than me, and I do not know him at all.

Yet I'm about to get in his car.

Technically it's a chauffeur-driven limo, but his car nonetheless.

He smiles as he guides me into the back seat before joining me.

"We don't have to stop anywhere if you don't want to. We'll go for a ride and if there's anything you want to see, tell me."

His voice is deep and gravelly, and I'm fascinated by the way his Adam's apple bobs when he speaks. He's wearing a collared shirt, but no tie, and his shirt has the top two buttons undone, giving me a glimpse of chest hair and tattoos.

I'm not stupid. I've read enough celebrity gossip to know he's bad news, but he's been nothing but helpful tonight, and even if Caitlin overdid it, there's no reason I can't have fun on my first and probably only trip to Vegas.

"That sounds great."

"I've told the driver to just drive around, and I'll let him know if we want to stop."

I nod. Now I'm here, my palms are sweaty. He makes me nervous because he's just so ... beautiful. When our eyes meet, his dark gaze pulls me in. I never understood the term 'movie star looks' before, but Declan embodies all that and then some. There's something glamorous about him—from that perfectly styled hair to the suit pants he's wearing. It's like he's stepped off a movie set.

The car pulls out from the kerb, and we're off to check out Sin City.

I'm well aware of the reputation Las Vegas has, but from the safety of the limo, I'm sheltered from any of the bad outside, and in my own little bubble watching the lights go by.

There are buildings I've only ever seen on television, or images Caitlin and I looked at while planning this trip. I gasp at the sight of the Sphinx lit up against the dark pyramid shape of the Luxor Hotel.

"What do you think?" he asks.

"It's very bright." I laugh, and he grins.

"How much electricity do you think they burn here?"

I shrug. "I'm just glad it's not *my* power bill."

Declan chuckles, and my heart leaps.

"You know, if we did this during the day there'd be so much more to see. We could go for a ride out to the Hoover Dam, or fly over the Grand Canyon."

I can't help but be excited at the thought. "Have you done that before?"

"Flown over the Grand Canyon?"

I nod.

"No. I've never done the tourist things here. I think this is the first time I've ever just driven around with no real destination in mind. It's a beautiful city." His dark-eyed gaze is fixed on me, and he reaches over and squeezes my knee. I catch my breath.

I reach up and cup his cheek. It's rough where his tightly trimmed beard ends.

"What *are* you doing?" His bemused tone makes me smile.

"You're so ... nice."

He raises his hand and lifts mine off his face and plants a kiss on my palm. "I can be very nice."

"I bet you can."

"Want a drink? There's plenty of champagne."

I frown. "I thought that was back in the suite."

"There's another bottle there. We might as well crack this open, too, given that I've already paid for it." He grins, and reaches into an ice bucket I hadn't spotted earlier, then pulls out a bottle.

I sigh contentedly and look back out the window as he pours two glasses before placing the bottle back.

"To our first tour of Las Vegas," he says.

With a giggle, I clink my glass against his.

I'm not even aware of it happening, but at some point I drift closer to him until his arms are around me and I'm leaning back against him. There's a lot to be said for cruising in a limo while sipping champagne.

This is the life.

"Do you come to Las Vegas often?" I ask.

"Only when I need to blow off some steam." His voice rumbles in my ear, and I sigh to myself.

"Thank you for tonight. I've had visiting here on my bucket list for a long time."

I barely notice the passing lights anymore as Declan talks about the places he seen in the world. I've only ever been in New Zealand and now the US, so I'm keen to see more of the country I consider my second home before I leave.

We're two glasses down when he makes a move, his lips brushing up my neck.

"Declan," I sigh.

"Tell me you want this too."

"Yes."

His hand slides up my leg, and I could curse myself for wearing pantyhose.

"Zoe. Are you okay with this? I need to touch you." His tone is urgent, his erection pressing against my lower back. He wants me as much as I want him, and I am so on for this.

"Yes." I'm breathless, turning my head again toward him as his mouth closes in on mine. He slides his hand higher on my thigh as his tongue skirts across my lips.

He tugs at my panties and pantyhose, slipping his hand inside, and I lean farther back to give him better access.

His long fingers slide over my clit.

"You're so wet," he whispers. "Is that all for me?"

I arch my back, rocking my hips, and pressing myself against him. "Yes."

"Jesus, woman." He laughs against my skin. "You'll have me coming in my pants like a teenager if you keep that up."

He slides two fingers inside me, and then back over my clit. I lean my head back on his shoulder.

I've never done anything so crazy—I'm a sit-in-front-of-the-TV-with-a-Milo-and-a-biscuit kind of girl. But right now,

I've got this beautiful man's fingers dipping in and out of me, and I close my eyes and ride the hell out of his hand.

"Zoe. Oh my god," he moans. His breath is hot behind my ear, and his other hand slides up my body until he's cupping my breast. My body's on fire from his touch, and I'm letting go in a way I've never done before.

My world explodes.

Waves of pleasure hit my body, and Declan claims my mouth, his hand moving up to my neck.

For the longest moment, I sit with my eyes closed as he peppers kisses on my face, still rocking gently against his hand as I ride out my orgasm.

"I want you inside me," I whisper.

"I need to take you back to my hotel room and finish this."

"Yes, please."

I've never been so forward, but after the champagne and the headiness of the night has loosened both of us up, I'm ready to make the most of my time here.

I'll never see this man again—never get the chance to spend the night with a movie star. My crazy life has just escalated.

Leaning over, he uses his free hand to press a button. "Back to the hotel please, Colin."

I lie against Declan, sated and boneless. I'm not even sure I can get out of the car if the drive isn't long.

"Are you okay?" he asks.

I breathe out a slow breath. "More than okay. It's been ... well, forever since I've done anything like this."

He chuckles.

"Okay, you got me," I continue. "I've never done anything like this."

His laughter comes to a stop. "What?"

"Oh, I'm not a virgin, but oh my god, Declan, that was amazing." I wouldn't normally talk so openly, but the wine has got to my tongue.

He wraps his arms around me and holds me tight. "I'm not letting you go tonight. That was just the start."

"What are you doing to me?"

The limo slows before coming to a stop, but he doesn't move, waiting until the driver opens the door to lift me to his side. He takes my hand and helps me out of the car, pulling me into his arms in the process.

"I got you," he murmurs.

It's warm, and he's wrapped around me, but I still shiver.

"You okay?"

"Can we go inside, please?"

He chuckles, then kisses me, long and deep. "The sooner I get you up to my room, the better."

With another kiss, we head inside, tangled in each other and laughing as we nearly trip over the other's feet.

Staggering into the elevator, I sigh as Declan keeps his arms around me and we snuggle into the corner while we ride all the way up to the suites. We're kissing as we make our way into his room, and when we step in, I pause and look around.

"I'm going to get us a drink," Declan says. "There are some bottles of water in the mini bar. I'll grab two of those."

"You promised me champagne."

He grins. "I did, but if you want to avoid a hangover …"

"I'll sleep all day tomorrow."

Shrugging, he turns toward the bar in the corner. "In that case, there's a bottle of champagne with our names on it."

I laugh as I make my way across the room toward the large windows.

It's crazy enough to be in Vegas, but the penthouse suite is a whole other level to the room I'm sharing with Caitlin. The lighting is low, and the view of The Strip below is full of vibrant, bright colour.

Declan stands behind the bar, pouring champagne as I stare out the window. I'm not sure I could ever live anywhere as busy and bright as Las Vegas, but I'm glad my trip out here wasn't a complete waste.

Caitlin is going to hate herself in the morning. We're here for one more night, but I think tomorrow will be quiet in comparison to this.

"The view is amazing, huh?" Declan approaches from behind and I turn to accept a champagne flute.

"Incredible."

"Looks pretty good from here too."

I turn. He's right behind me, and he leans down to nuzzle my neck. He cups my right breast with his free hand and my nipples get up and dance in response.

I want him.

But even after coming all over his hand in the limo, I'm a little uncertain—even shy. I'm the type of person who usually keeps to herself. Caitlin and I met when I ventured out of my apartment for a meal and a drink, and she's so confident that she inserted herself into my life at first. It turned out we were neighbours. If she hadn't forced the issue, I would be a recluse, happy in my apartment writing code and making apps. But I'm glad she did—and not just because it led me here.

He takes me by the hand and leads me to the couch where he pulls me down onto his lap.

"One drink, and then we'll take the bottle to bed," he says.

"I like that idea."

We clink our glasses together.

"So, what are you doing in Vegas?" I ask.

"Like I told you earlier, letting off steam." He sits beside me, stretching his long legs out, and then takes a sip of his drink. "I'm retiring from acting."

"Whoa." I twist toward him, propping myself against the back of the couch with my elbow. "That's a big decision. You're not *that* old."

He chuckles. "I'm done. My career's in the crapper, and I'd like to get out with some dignity."

"I'm sorry."

Regret flickers across his features, but it's gone as fast as it arrives. "I'm ready to move on. But I'm not sure what I'm going to do. How about you? You mentioned maybe going back to New Zealand?"

I nod. "I'm two years into a three year contract. Once that's up, I'm not sure what I'm doing next. I'm not sure whether I should find something else to do here, or go home."

His smile is lopsided. "I'm not a good source for advice— if I knew what I was doing, I wouldn't be in the position I'm in. But if I were you, I'd look at all the pros and cons of either decision."

"Is that what you did when you decided to retire?"

He places his glass on the coffee table.

"In a way. I just made a movie with some crazy talented people, and it'll barely see the light of day. No premiere, no chance of winning any awards. I cash the cheque and it'll sink like a stone." He sighs. "I don't want to do that anymore. I want to be happy again."

He takes my champagne flute from me and places it on the coffee table, along with his own.

My heart thuds.

He turns back, the desire in his eyes making my throat tighten.

I want him, and he wants me. That much is obvious. Should I be doing this while my friend's sleeping off the booze downstairs? Probably not. But she's safe where she is, and it's been forever since I've had sex.

"You're so gorgeous," he whispers. "I wanted you the minute I saw you."

His lips crash down onto mine, and I'm done.

My first one-night stand is coming right up. I know that's all it'll ever be—that's the kind of thing a man like him does. And even though it's not what I usually do, I'm about to break every rule in my book for him.

He rests his hand just below my breast as he kisses me again, and I place my fingers over his and slide it up until he's cupping me just below my nipple.

"Are you sure?" he asks.

"I want you." I'm breathless. "I've never had a one-night stand, and I'm sure that's all you want, but I'm ready."

He squeezes my breast in response before kissing me again. I close my eyes, losing myself in the kiss of a man who knows what to do with his tongue.

That thought excites me even more.

The things this man can do with my body ...

He runs his tongue up the side of my neck before nibbling on my earlobe. My eyelids flutter.

"I want to taste every single inch of you," he murmurs.

I lean back while he drops to the floor in front of me. This time, he finds a small hole in my pantyhose. He tears the crotch open, and the cooler air of the room flows through

His dark eyes meet mine, and I grip the couch, willing him to make his next move.

After sliding my panties to the side, he pushes a finger inside me, never breaking eye contact. He inserts another finger and then slowly pumps them in and out of me before leaning over and placing a soft kiss on my thigh.

"I can smell your pussy, Zoe. I want to taste it so badly. How many times do you think I can make you come?"

"I don't know." I whimper.

He pushes his head up my dress until he places a kiss right next to my pussy. I shuffle forward in the hopes he'll touch my clit. He chuckles, his hot breath on my sensitive core makes me moan.

"So impatient," he murmurs.

"I only have one night."

He kisses my thigh again, and then raises his head to grin at me. "It's still early. We have plenty of time."

Sliding my panties farther to one side, he pumps his fingers again before lowering his mouth to my clit. The touch of his tongue leaves me panting.

He slides his fingers out and raises them to his mouth. I can't take my eyes off him as he swirls his tongue around the tips before sucking on them. "You taste as good as you smell."

Standing, he holds out his hand.

I giggle, taking it, and he helps me up and into his arms.

"Bedroom?" he asks.

"Yes, please. I think I can walk."

He frowns. "You're not *that* drunk, are you?"

"I'm fine. Just legless thinking about the insane orgasm you're about to give me."

Laughing, he leads me into the bedroom where the biggest bed I've ever seen is waiting. I sigh, staring at the mattress that has to have been specially ordered. Surely they don't make them that big.

"I could get lost in that."

He pulls me to him, kissing me deeply. "I'd come searching."

I drop onto the bed, laughing as I bounce. He leans over and kisses me again.

"I need you," I whisper.

He kicks off his shoes before toeing off his socks.

His shirt comes off next, and I stop everything just to watch. I raise my hands as the urge to touch his chiselled chest becomes overwhelming, but he's already working on the waist of his dress pants, undoing the button and sliding the zip down to reveal boxer shorts underneath.

And then, without a sliver of humility, he drops the boxers and stands before me, naked and erect.

I've never been an admirer of cocks, but Declan's is both impressive and beautiful. He's long and thick, and my insides ache just thinking of him pulsing in and out of my pussy.

He chuckles and reaches over, wiping the drool from beneath my bottom lip. "Like what you see?"

I'm almost panting. "I love it."

"I need to get you naked, Zoe."

His deep voice sends shivers down my spine, and I stand, reaching for the hem of my dress then tugging it over my head.

Declan drops to his knees in front of me, gripping my arse with his large hands, and planting a kiss on my belly button. He tugs my panties and what remains of my pantyhose down to my ankles, removing them along with my shoes before trailing his tongue down to my pussy and lifting one of my legs over his shoulder.

And then he feasts.

I close my eyes, my hips grinding against his face as he teases my clit with his tongue. He's so good at it, and I get lost in the sensation, losing all track of time. But before I come, he rises, scooping me into his arms and depositing me on the bed.

The man's a work of art.

He's all muscle with a smattering of chest hair at the top and a happy trail that leads … I can't think about that right now.

But I do want to run my tongue over those tattoos on his chest.

The smirk on his lips just makes him even more attractive.

He lowers his head and kisses me gently.

I want more.

As he deepens the kiss, I roll with him until we're facing each other.

"You're so beautiful. I'm a lucky man." He unclips my bra and drags it down my arms.

He kisses me again, running a hand along my spine. His hard cock presses against my pussy, and I don't care about anything other than having him inside me.

I reach out tentatively, but he places his hand on mine until I have a firm hold of his shoulder. The muscle flexes under my touch as he lowers his head to take one nipple into his mouth. His tongue's rough against my sensitive bud, and I can't get enough of it.

I cradle his head in my hands, running my fingers through his hair.

He rolls me onto my back, then slides his way down my body until he's hovering over my pussy again.

Without a word, he's back into it, his mouth and tongue working me over, but this time he lets me crest the wave, my body bucking as hot waves of pleasure overtake me.

I pant for a moment while trying to catch my breath.

The wooden scrape of the bedside cabinet drawer opening turns my head.

My cheeks burn when Declan pulls a strip of condoms out. Is this why he's here? Just to get laid? I guess it makes sense—and it's what I want from him, after all, but the dose of reality hits me hard.

"There are a few condoms there."

Declan pulls one off the strip. "I bought them just in case."

I bite my bottom lip.

"Zoe, if you're not comfortable and want to stop—"

"Don't you dare." It only takes a moment for me to realise I don't care. "Fuck me."

He grins before kissing me again. After tearing open the condom, he rolls it down his cock.

Lowering himself down onto me, he kisses me again while he slides himself inside my pussy.

I pant against his mouth.

He chuckles. "Love the way you feel, babe. Perfect."

Propping himself up on his arms, he moves, and I meet each thrust with my hips, pushing him in deeper. I want every little piece of him I can get.

"Not so fast. I want to last," he murmurs. "Keep doing that and I'll embarrass myself."

"You could never do that," I whisper. "And if you did, it just means we'd have to do it all over again."

Declan laughs as he pulls me with him until I'm straddling his hips.

"Ride me, gorgeous," he says, his large hands resting on my butt.

I throw my head back and roll my hips. I've never been so uninhibited. The bright lights of Las Vegas illuminate the room, and although no one can see us, the open curtains leave me feeling like an exhibitionist.

Declan thrusts up, deep inside me.

"You're beautiful, Zoe," he murmurs. "So tight and hot."

Running one hand up my back, he pulls me down toward him then sucks a nipple into his mouth and makes me gasp.

"You feel so good." I grind against him, lost in sensation, his thumb strumming my clit as he coaxes another orgasm out of me.

We fall together, his loud groan coming at the same time as his name from my lips.

Perfect.

THREE
ZOE

A WARM BODY with a hard chest is pressed against my back. I sigh with contentment before my brain catches up and ...

What did I do last night?

I wasn't that drunk.

Oh crap. Caitlin was. I remember getting her back to our room, and then ...

He moves behind me, raising his hand to my breast and giving it a squeeze. His lips press against the nape of my neck. "Good morning."

That voice. It's not enough that Declan O'Leary has those movie-star looks. His voice is all deep and gravelly, and sexy as sin.

He slides his other hand down my thigh and between my legs. The man's insatiable, but I'm not complaining.

"Morning," I whisper. My stomach gurgles, and I let out a laugh.

"Hungry?" he asks, his index finger sliding over my clit.

I let out a sigh, arching my back as he gently bites my shoulder. My head's still fuzzy from last night, but I want him. "A little."

"I want you for breakfast." He chuckles, and slips his finger into me. I have no shame. The man makes me want more, even when we barely know one another.

He barely needs to do anything. I roll my hips and rub myself against his hand. My body heats as I ride his fingers to find my own pleasure before he pulls me onto my back.

"Give me something to remember our night together." I laugh.

His eyes darken. "I think I can do that."

Maybe it's because he's so damn good at it. But every nerve in my body is alive, and Declan has a magic tongue.

He slides his hands under my arse and grips it, pulling me tight against his face as he devours me. I don't ever want to get out of bed.

Two orgasms later, he slides into me. I close my eyes, basking in his attentions as he caresses my body. It's like he's trying to remember every inch of it before our time together comes to an end.

Oh, how I love his touch.

He slips his hand between us, coaxing one more orgasm out of my body right as he shudders, pulsing inside me.

My stomach rumbles a second time, and I giggle.

"It's time I fed you," he says. "Although I know that means I'm one step closer to letting you go."

I brush my fingers against his cheek. This man. He

doesn't need to be so sweet given that we're not likely to ever see each other again, but it's nice.

Another kiss, and he's out of bed. I miss his warmth the second he leaves.

But he's only gone a moment.

I stretch and yawn as he walks back into the room.

"Food is on its way."

"I need coffee. Lots and lots of coffee."

He makes his way to my side of the bed until he's standing over me. His eyes drink me in, and he reaches down to rub my shoulder. "Feeling seedy?"

"A little. Something to eat and lots of water and I'll come right." I raise my face to look at him, and he leans over and kisses me.

I don't want this to end.

The way he kisses me, I don't think he does either as he lingers on my lips.

"I should get dressed," I say.

He lets out a sigh, running his gaze down my bare breasts. "It's such a shame to, but yes. Come and get some breakfast when you're ready."

It's an impressive sight watching Declan round the bed to grab his boxer shorts, still as naked and unashamed as he was last night. I know he's older than me—how much older I'm not sure, but he's so cut and I feel out of shape in comparison.

But the way he looks at me, I feel like a queen.

It's not much fun sliding my dress from the night before over my head, and I tuck my panties and pantyhose into my clutch rather than put them back on again. but by the time

I'm dressed and out of the bedroom, the food has arrived and the familiar aroma of toast makes my stomach grumble.

I'm surprised I'm not feeling worse, but then again ...

Caitlin.

I grimace. She'll be a hot mess today.

She'll also wonder where I am if she's awake.

I flick her a quick text.

Me: *Just having breakfast and I'll be back*

Declan looks up as I approach the table and smiles.

"I figured we needed something basic, so there's toast. How do you take your coffee?"

"White. One sugar. Thank you." I drop my clutch on the table and take a seat.

That first mouthful of buttered toast is divine, and I moan.

"Keep that up and we'll be back in that bed." Declan winks at me and I smile.

"Thank you for last night. It was wonderful."

"You're very welcome. I was wondering ..." He looks away as if he's embarrassed. This is insane. I'm the one who should be all shy and retiring. I've heard stories about Declan O'Leary—seen him on magazine covers. He parties.

"Wondering what?"

"If I could use your number sometime."

I swallow hard. Do I tell him that last night is quite fuzzy? I don't want him to think he took advantage of me—I knew what I wanted as much as he did. And I know the sex was amazing, but I can't remember the finer details of what happened between us.

"Sure." He must say this to all the women he's with. Maybe it's the easiest way to get them to sign an NDA.

He takes a sip of his coffee before slowly placing the cup back on the table. "I'm no good at this. I'm the last person you want to get entangled with. I can't make any promises," he says.

I reach across and place my hand on his. "I get it. And I'm good. If this is all this is, then I'll have the memory of getting my brains fucked out by a movie star."

Declan chuckles. "I hope you think more of me than that."

"Of course I do. What you are doesn't matter to me. Who you are does."

He rolls his eyes. "That sounds like a line."

"Maybe it does, but it's true."

His eyebrows twitch as he gazes at me. "I don't know if anyone's ever said anything like that to me before."

I frown before standing and make my way around to his side of the table. He grins as he pushes back his chair and I drop onto his lap. "You're more than your job, Declan. I spent the night with you because I think you're hot—not because you're in movies."

His eyes flash with amusement. "You think I'm hot."

I run my fingers through his hair. "Who wouldn't? I'm not some silly starstruck girl."

He studies me intently. "No, no you're not."

"Thank you. For everything."

"Oh, you are very welcome." He smirks. "But I should be thanking you. I came here to have one last blow-out before I reset my life. I thought my night would be more like Caitlin's was than the night we shared."

"Really?"

His eyes search mine. "I don't know what my future looks like, but I'm glad I found you last night."

I slap his shoulder. "Don't you go getting all sentimental on me."

"I'll treasure our time together forever, Zoe. Now go on and do great things with your life."

Oh, he's not going to call me.

Did he suggest he would to soften the blow of this being a one-night stand?

If we had more time together, I'd tell him what I've done so far—that I've done great things and now I'm trying to work out what does come next. But that's not a conversation to be had today.

"Right back at you," I whisper.

He grips my arse and kisses me softly. "I don't want to cut this even shorter, but I'm checking out today."

I nod. "I get it."

He gives me one more lingering kiss before I leave.

As I step outside his room, I look down at how I'm dressed. I'm still wearing my little black dress from the night before.

I'm doing the walk of shame.

However, once I get in the elevator and it starts to move down toward my floor, stopping every so often to pick up other guests, I realise that in a Las Vegas casino, people are gambling at all hours of the day and night, which means my clothing doesn't stand out among everyone else's. For all they know, I've been sitting beside a slot machine for hours.

I reach my floor and sigh. Declan and I'll only ever have one night, but I can't help but feel I've left a part of my heart in that hotel suite.

It's with great reluctance that I make my way back to our hotel room.

Maybe Caitlin messed up her weekend, but mine has been unforgettable. Even if last night is a little hazy.

I swipe the card and let myself in. The room's dark, and I turn on the lamp beside my bed. The gentle light doesn't do much to illuminate the room, but it gives me enough visibility to see the lump in the bed next to mine.

"Caitlin?" I whisper.

A long, loud moan comes from the bed, and I clamp my lips together to stop myself from laughing. I'd thought I'd had a heavy night, but apparently that was nothing compared to my best friend's.

"That bad, huh?" I finally say.

"I think a herd of stampeding elephants have set up home in my brain." She rolls over, flicking on her bedside light, and I can't help it—I bark out a laugh that makes her wince.

If she'd been more with it, I might have helped her take her makeup off before she fell asleep, but now her mascara is smeared, and her hair looks like she's stuck her finger in an electrical socket.

"Just as well we're not going home today. I don't think you could handle that." I tilt my head.

She rubs her face with her hands. "God no. Any turbulence and I'll be hurling all over the cabin."

I bite my bottom lip to stop myself from laughing more. "I've had breakfast. Do you want anything?"

"The thought of food makes me want to puke."

I nod slowly. "Fair enough. How about coffee? And a big bottle of water."

She opens one eye. "Never mind that. Where have you been?"

I sit on her bed and grin. "Oh, I've got a story to tell you."

"Is it anything to do with where you've been all night? You weren't here when I woke up stupidly early, so I assume you've been up to no good."

My cheeks flush red, and her mouth drops open. "You could say that."

"Well, woman. Spill the beans."

I draw in a deep breath. "After we left you here, Declan called his car and we went for a drive around Vegas. We didn't really stop anywhere, but I got to see so much—"

Caitlin's hand lands on my arm. "Can we please get to the dirty bits?"

I snort. "Is that all you want from me?"

She lets out a yawn. "I had too much to drink and went to sleep early. You spent the night with a movie star, and I want to know everything. Please, Zoe. I need some excitement in my weekend."

Biting my lip, I hold up four fingers.

Her eyes widen. "Four times? You did it four times?"

"Three last night and once this morning before breakfast."

She smiles. "You look happy, and I love it. This is out of character, but so good for you. You're glowing."

I sigh with contentment. "It was really good. He's amazing."

"I'm glad you had a good night." She raises her arm to cover her face. "I'm an idiot."

I shake my head. "No, you're not. You're happy and excited, and you got carried away. We'll just have a quiet night tonight. I'll order you some breakfast. You need to eat something."

Patting her on the hand, I move to the couch and pick up the phone. After ordering some French toast and coffee, I close my eyes and smile at the thought of last night.

My body hums at the memory of Declan's touch. That man knows how to make a girl happy. I'm going to eat out on that memory for months if not years.

And speaking of eating out …

I've never known a man who enjoys oral sex the way Declan does.

I get so lost in my thoughts I nearly miss the quiet tap on the door.

"Caitlin, food's here."

"Can you not be so loud?" she grumbles.

Once the food's delivered, I tip the waiter and roll the cart closer to our table before moving the food. I ordered two lattes with triple shots for each of us, and I breathe in the aroma.

Banging and crashing sounds come from the bathroom, and I snort with laughter as Caitlin emerges. Her panda eyes are gone, and her hair isn't so wild, but she still looks as if she needs more sleep.

"That coffee smells amazing." She walks to the table. "My

stomach is doing flips though. I'm not sure how much I can eat."

I sit on the other side of the table to her. "Get a couple of bites in and it might make you feel well enough to eat the rest. You know it's what you need."

"Thanks, Mom." She drops into the seat and sighs. "How are you not hungover?"

"I am. I'm just not as bad as you. I'll have an early night tonight."

She lets out a groan. "I don't want to eat this."

"It'll make you feel better."

Her gaze doesn't drop from mine as she grimaces and then lifts up her toast. I snicker at her extreme facial expressions when she takes exaggerated bites and then winces.

"You're such a drama queen." I throw a napkin at her.

"I'm allowed to be." She pouts. "I'm losing my freedom in two weeks, and I just screwed up my last weekend away."

I snort. "I thought it was Brandon who was supposed to be going on about losing his freedom. Isn't that what men do?"

She laughs. "Ignore me. I'm just feeling sorry for myself. Especially after the night you had. I could have been cruising around Vegas with Declan O'Leary."

Sitting in the back seat of that car watching the bright lights go past, moving in close against Declan, his arm around me ...

"Zoe? Are you even listening to me?"

I blink rapidly. "What?"

"You're so preoccupied. Was he that good?"

I smirk. "I think my vagina needs a holiday to recover from our weekend break."

Caitlin rolls her eyes. "Stop rubbing it in. My mom is going to be so jealous."

I smile to myself.

"How lucky are you though?" Caitlin continues. "A one-night stand with a sexy movie star." She sighs.

"He said he might call me sometime."

Her eyes widen. "No way."

"Yes way. I could always call him. I've got his number too."

Caitlin lies back on the couch. "Lucky bitch."

I laugh. "You know it."

"Are you going to call him?"

I swallow hard. That's the thing about swapping numbers. Would he reject me if I called?

"We'll see." I blow out a breath. "Can we just not talk about this again? It's not that I want to forget it, but this whole thing is out of character for me, and I'm not ashamed of it, but it's personal."

Caitlin leans over and places her hand on mine "Of course. Whatever you want." Her blue eyes disarm me. "I bet he fucks like a beast."

I snort. "You *are* feeling better."

FOUR

ZOE

Two weeks later

I TWIRL my straw around in my drink and force a smile.

As much as I love Caitlin, it feels a little like I've been thrown to the wolves at her wedding reception, having already fended off Brandon's best man, Eric.

It was a beautiful ceremony, but I'm glad the reception is nearly over.

I have to physically stop myself from rolling my eyes as Brandon's younger brother, Lachlan, comes stumbling toward me. It's been a very boozy reception, although I nursed my first glass of champagne so it lasted for half the night, and now I'm really glad I made that decision. I'm clear-headed when everyone around me is a mess.

"So, you're Caitlin's friend." His slur makes his words almost unrecognisable.

"Yeah."

"Wanna fuck?"

I recoil at the combined aromas of alcohol and cigarette smoke belching from him as he leans forward.

"God no." Turning my head, I hold up my palm against him.

"Oh, come on. Brandon said you were into one-night stands. You had one a couple of weeks ago. I'm not looking for a girlfriend."

Anger builds in me. So much for what happens in Vegas stays in Vegas. Besides which, Lachlan making the assumption that I'm going to have a one-night stand with him because I've had one with someone else is gross. "Brandon got it wrong."

He grasps my forearm, and the glass of lemonade in my hand spills over and onto my skirt.

"Come on, Zoe. It's just a bit of fun."

"Go find your fun somewhere else, Lachlan. I'm not interested."

Switching my drink to my other hand, I shake off his grip and stalk toward Caitlin. She smiles brightly as I approach her, and I draw in a deep breath.

"You told Brandon about my one-night stand in Vegas?" I'm sure my eyes are bugging out of my head as I vent.

Caitlin grimaces. "Not deliberately. We were talking about the weekend, and I let it slip. I'm sorry."

"Well, Brandon has a big mouth and told Lachlan about

it. And Eric. And God only knows who else. I'm done with getting hit on because of it."

She frowns. "He promised ..."

"Yeah, well he broke his promise."

Her eyes flick away from my face, and she seems to scan the room before she narrows them. I don't have to look to know she's giving Brandon a death stare.

I drop down onto a chair and she follows suit beside me.

She leans her head on my arm. "I'm sorry, Zoe. I never meant to hurt you. You know I love you like a sister."

I sigh. "It's okay. It just hate how it turned something exciting into something almost shameful. I shouldn't be made to feel that way.

"It's very unlike you. I guess that's why it stands out. But you're right. I'm glad you let loose. It's not like you do it very often ..." She raises her head and meets my gaze. "Has he called yet?"

I shake my head. "Not a word. I didn't really expect him to. It was surprising enough that he took my number."

"Then he doesn't deserve you." She smiles. "And neither do any of these assholes."

"That's Brandon's friends and family you're talking about."

She sighs. "I know, but I also know Brandon will go nuts if I tell him what happened with Lachlan. He never would have wanted to hurt you either."

I peck her on the cheek then rest my head against hers. "Don't say anything. At least while you're on honeymoon. I want you two to have fun."

"Oh we'll have that regardless." She giggles. "I'm sorry he didn't call you."

I shrug and straighten up. "Me too. We were really good together. But let's face it. He's way out of my league."

Caitlin takes my hand in hers. "No way. He would have been the luckiest man alive to have you. It's his loss."

I groan as Brandon approaches. Sure enough, he wants to know what that dirty look was for, judging from the quizzical expression on his face.

"Babe? You okay?"

Caitlin shakes her head. "No. Tell your boys to stop hitting on Zoe. She's not interested."

He frowns. "Who? I'll take care of it."

I sigh. "It doesn't matter."

Brandon sits beside Caitlin. "Tell me who it is, and I'll beat the shit out of them."

She wraps herself around him. "My hero."

"It's not worth it. Today is supposed to be about love and fun," I say.

He plants a kiss on Caitlin's temple. "Speaking of, we need to get out of here."

"I love you guys. Have an amazing honeymoon, and we'll catch up when you get back." I squeeze her knee.

"Love you too," Caitlin says.

"I'm sorry the guys have been harassing you." Brandon frowns. "I'll deal with them when I'm home again."

"I'm fine. I think everyone just needs to sleep it off."

He nods. With one last hug, they leave, waving goodbye to everyone as they make their way out to the car. I'm not sure it's sunk in just how much our lives are about to change. With

Brandon being traded to Chicago, Caitlin will be right behind him in a few weeks.

It's a long trek back to my hotel room. I'm so happy for Caitlin, and I hope she has a wonderful honeymoon. Today just emphasises the fact that I'm alone—if I only wanted sex, I would've taken up Lachlan or someone else's proposition tonight.

But now I'm not sure anyone can top Declan O'Leary. It's gonna take a very long time to get over that night together. Since that weekend, my memory has become a little hazy. I know the sex was amazing, and I definitely remember what happened before breakfast the following morning. But I wish now I hadn't had anything to drink and had had a completely clear head.

Maybe if I called him …

I curl up in my bed and think about what might have been.

No. That's not fair.

Declan O'Leary is a pipe dream. Maybe we had that night together, but I'll never see him in the flesh again.

All I have left is my murky memory.

FIVE
ZOE

Six weeks later

I PICK up my phone for approximately the one millionth time since our weekend in Vegas.

Declan never called me.

And I'm too stubborn to call him.

With me only being here until the end of the year, it might not be the best idea to start a new romance anyway. When I sold, the contract for the deal contained a clause for me to stay on and help manage the transition to the new owner's infrastructure. Every day I have less and less to do—my time with the company was planned that way as I ease myself out of it.

The deal was so big, once I work out this year I never have to work again, but there's also a sense of loss that what was once mine is gone. If I want to build something new, I'll have to start all over again.

I knew all this when I sold my company, but the closer I get to the conclusion of my contract, the more adrift I feel.

"What's crawled up your ass?" Caitlin asks.

Brandon is out with friends, and I invited her over to hang out. She's leaving in a couple of days, but now I'm regretting hosting her. I'm not feeling great, and I'm cranky as hell. She's not done anything wrong, but the last thing I want is for her to cop it just because I'm grumpy.

"Nothing."

"He hasn't called yet? What a prick." She's on my side—I know that, but everything is grating on me right now and her words still irritate me.

"Maybe he's busy."

"For eight weeks?" She frowns. "I'm sorry, Zoe, but the guy's an asshole. He should never have asked for your number and given you hope." I burst into tears, and her sad expression changes to one of horror.

"I know all that. It's just ..." I sniff.

"What's going on?" Her soft tone makes everything worse.

"I don't know. I'm getting closer to the end of my contract, and you're moving, and everything's a mess." I fling my hands up to add melodramatic flair.

She bites her lower lip before resting her hand on my arm. "Don't take this the wrong way ..."

My eyebrows rise. "What?"

"Have you thought about taking a pregnancy test?"

I shoot her the side-eye. "Why would I do that?"

"Because you're grumpy all the time, and you were a little green around the gills when we had breakfast the other day. You're just not yourself."

"I'm not pregnant." I huff.

"Go and buy a test. It's not like it's far to get one. There's a pharmacy ..."

"I know where it is."

She shoots to her feet. "Fine. I'll go buy one now."

"Don't. I'll get one. Just not this instant."

Before I can stop her, she's grabbed her bag and flung her coat over her shoulders, and is stamping toward the door.

I'm not sure how long I sit there, frozen by uncertainty until she storms back in, slamming the door in her wake and waving a small blue box at me.

"You owe me."

I laugh. "What are you talking about?"

"The woman at Walgreens recognised me. She's a big Brandon fan. Now there'll be rumours about me being pregnant." She flicks her blonde locks over her shoulder.

"Well, if I remember rightly, I told you not to go out and get a test. It's your own fault."

She wriggles out of her coat and throws it on a nearby chair. "Now I've gone to all that trouble, you can go and take the test."

I shake my head. "You're a pain in the arse."

"You'll miss me when I'm gone."

My throat tightens. I will miss her. Regardless of what happens, we'll be in different parts of the world and not in each other's pockets like we have been these past two years.

How quickly Caitlin has become such a big part of my

life—one I'm going to struggle to do without. When I first came to the US, I had no one. I've got friends back home, but none I would call my best friend.

She frowns.

"I will miss you." I sniff.

"I'll miss you too. But I'm only at the end of the phone. So before I sail off into the sunset, I want you to take that test."

I sigh. "I'll miss your bossiness. And okay. I'll take the damn test, but I'm telling you, it'll be negative."

Caitlin pats me on the head. "Good girl."

I snatch it out of her hand. "Wait here. I want to at least pee in private."

Her laughter follows me all the way to the bathroom. She's right. I do need to do this. It's all adding up. I'm terrible at tracking my cycle. If Caitlin hadn't said anything, I probably wouldn't have realised that I haven't had my period in ... how long has it been?

I glare at the blue box before ripping it open and pulling out the stick.

"You'd better only have one line," I grumble.

It only takes a moment to do the test, but the instructions say now I need to wait. Doubt starts to creep in as I place the test on the bathroom cabinet. Could I be pregnant?

I do know we used condoms—I remember that much, plus I'm on birth control pills. But nothing's one hundred per cent, and we did have sex multiple times.

And I'm sure I haven't had my period since before our trip.

Oh God. I am pregnant.

I don't even need to check the test to know.

The one night I kicked loose and acted out of character, I ended up pregnant. It's also not like Declan and I will ever be in a relationship—his past speaks for itself.

It was just one night.

I wipe myself clean and pull up my panties, sitting on the toilet again for a moment before taking a deep breath and picking up the test.

Two pink lines.

For a moment, I just sit there. There's nothing else I can do.

Declan O'Leary knocked me up and never called me.

What an asshole.

I glower at the test in my hand before slamming it down on the counter. Standing, I wash my hands, then pick the test back up to show Caitlin.

Her eyes widen when she takes the sight of me in.

"This is your fault." I wave the test at her.

"Wait. What? What's happened?" She grabs hold of my arm, and her mouth falls open as she stares at the plastic white stick. "Shit."

"How the hell did this happen?"

Caitlin cocks her head. "Well, it usually happens when a penis is inserted into a vagina and ..."

"This isn't funny." I frown again at the two pink lines on the white stick in front of me.

She slips her arm around my shoulders and I rest my head against hers. "There's no way it's not Declan's?"

"Has to be his. I haven't had sex with anyone else in months. Unless it's an immaculate conception, the father is Declan O'Leary."

"My mom loves him," she says in a dreamy voice.

"That's not helpful," I snap.

She lets out a sigh and squeezes my shoulder. "Why don't we talk this out. Are you going to keep it?"

"I only just did the test—I haven't got that far." Knitting my fingers together, I raise my knuckles to my lips. What the hell *am* I going to do? "I need to tell him."

"Why?" she scoffs. "It's not like he's going to want it."

"Maybe, but he's still the father, and if he or she wants to know about their dad later on, I'd much rather he knows."

"So, you're keeping it." She chuckles and places a kiss on my temple. "Whatever you do, you know you have me. I'm always a hundred per cent behind you. I just don't want you to rush into any rash decisions."

I sigh. "He gave me his number. I guess I'll call him."

She nods. "Do you need me to sit with you? Moral support?"

"No. I'll be fine. Thank you." I give her hand a squeeze.

"You're never alone, Zoe. You've always got me."

"You're leaving."

"And your contract is up at the end of the year. You could always come to Chicago. And even if I'm not always physically with you, I'm just at the end of the phone or we can Zoom."

There's so much to think about. I can't say it to Caitlin, but a big part of me just wants to crawl home to New Zealand and back to Mum and Dad. I'll have to organise a meeting with Jason and Chrissie—the people who bought my company to discuss this pregnancy, but there's nothing stopping me working for as long as I can and then being available for support.

Caitlin being my best friend is the only other thing that's kept me here.

And now she's spreading her wings.

It's time to spread my wings too.

Her phone pings, and she rolls her eyes.

"Let me guess. It's your husband." I don't mean it as down as it comes out. Brandon has been nothing but good to me.

"We've got reservations. I need to go home and get changed, and I'm already running late."

I stare at her. "This could have waited."

"No, it really couldn't. Besides, you're important. You always will be. I don't want you to forget that."

Tears well in my eyes. "I won't forget. You're important to me too."

"Love you." She plants a kiss on my temple.

I sniff. "Love you right back."

"See you later?"

The concern in her eyes makes me want to reassure her, but I can't when I'm so uncertain. How will Declan take my news?

Does it really matter?

I'm thirty years old. If I'm going to have a baby, it might as well be now. Who knows what the future will bring when it comes to having a family? I'm not short of money—the whole reason I'm in the US is because I sold my business to an American one.

I can do this without Declan.

But I'm still going to tell him.

"Zoe?" Caitlin pinches my bicep.

"Ouch." I glare at Caitlin and rub my arm. "What was that for?"

"You were miles away. I can call Brandon and let him know I'm staying longer if you need me."

I shake my head. "No. You go and have a great evening. I'll be fine."

She lingers for a moment, her brow still furrowed. "Call me if you need me."

"I will." I grasp her forearm. "Seriously, I'm all good. I'll call Declan to make a time to go and see him. If he doesn't want to meet, then I'll be okay."

I know she doesn't like me doing this alone, but if I'm raising this baby without Declan, I need to get used to doing things by myself.

Before I come up with a million reasons not to tell him, I have to pull up my big girl panties and make that call.

It's not until Caitlin's gone that I pick up my phone. My finger hovers over Declan's contact before I take a deep breath and tap it.

"Hello." Weeks have passed, but his deep, sexy voice takes me back to the hotel room.

I swallow hard. "Declan, it's Zoe."

"Zoe?" He pauses for a moment. "Las Vegas Zoe?"

I bite my bottom lip. He remembers me at least. "That's me. Las Vegas Zoe." I laugh.

"What can I do for you?" His tone makes it sound like he's on edge—suspicious. I'm not really surprised. He's famous and people undoubtedly approach him for all kinds of things.

"I'm coming to Los Angeles, and I wondered if we could get together for a coffee? There's something we need to discuss."

There's silence, and I assume he's digesting my words. There aren't many things we'd have to talk about, so he's got to guess what I'm calling about. But I don't want to do this over the phone. If we're going to discuss things, I want it done face-to-face.

"Sure. Text me the place and time and I'll be there."

A sense of relief washes over me. I'd thought he might be difficult—he might still be difficult, but he's prepared to meet me and that's a start.

I don't need a man in my life. I'm perfectly capable of raising a child by myself. But the combination of not wanting to have secrets and the raging hormones inside me are forcing my hand.

"Thanks, Declan."

"Are you okay, sweetheart?"

I blink rapidly and shift my gaze to the ceiling in an attempt not to cry. "I'm fine."

"Let me know when you get into town. I'm not working, so I'm free any time." His soft tone takes me by surprise, and I smile to myself.

"Okay. Thanks. Talk soon."

SIX
DECLAN

FOR THE PAST two month I've thought about Zoe so many times.

I'm making a fresh start. Why can't that include the woman who turned everything upside down in Las Vegas?

I'd thought I'd be there to party, but instead I'd found an unforgettable woman—one I'm too chicken to call.

The simple reality is that I have nothing to offer her.

Sure, I have money, but a woman like Zoe deserves the world. She deserves a man who hasn't had such a messy past—one who can commit to her and keep his promises.

I'm not sure I can be that man.

But oh how I want to be.

And the whole time Nikki's been blowing up my phone. I get it. She doesn't want to lose a client like me. Even as my career tanked, my paydays were decent enough. But I just can't do it anymore.

I haven't had a holiday in years. Although I'm certain I'm done, the least I need is a break.

When the phone rings, I blow out a long, frustrated breath. Nikki's the only person who's been calling, so when I pick up and see Zoe's name, I arch an eyebrow.

I pause before tapping accept. "Hello."

"Declan, it's Zoe."

"Zoe?" *Gotta play it cool.* "Las Vegas Zoe?"

"That's me. Las Vegas Zoe." She laughs.

Wait. What's she calling for? It's been … two months.

My stomach sinks.

She couldn't be … could she?

"What can I do for you?"

"I'm coming to Los Angeles and I wondered if we could get together for a coffee? There's something we need to discuss."

Shit.

I've had this conversation before. She's pregnant. Last time, I was so drunk I couldn't remember fucking the woman claiming she was having my baby. It turned out that that was because I hadn't. She was in the right place at the right time, but on that occasion I'd had too much to perform.

But because she ticked two of those boxes, I'd still had to go through the whole paternity test thing and wait to make sure.

This time I have a clear memory of being with Zoe. The way her body moulded to mine, her response to every touch, and the way she tasted. Also, the way we used protection—we were safe. I made sure of it.

"Sure. Text me the place and time, and I'll be there." I'm

short with her—I know I am, but I'm not sure how to feel. Was this her plan all along?

"Thanks, Declan," she says, and her voice sounds so sad.

I hate it when women cry—especially the ones I like. And yep, despite my inner turmoil, I like the woman. I can't help it.

"Are you okay, sweetheart?"

There's a pause before she responds, which makes my suspicions for why she's calling a little more likely. "I'm fine."

"Let me know when you get into town. I'm not working, so I'm free any time." I want to see her—want to lay eyes on her again, and hear the words from her lips.

"Okay. Thanks. Talk soon."

And then she's gone, and I'm left in the quiet of this stupidly big house all alone in the Hollywood Hills.

I guess all I do now is wait.

TWO DAYS LATER, I get the text with a location, date, and time to meet Zoe.

I make sure I get there early, order coffee, and find the most discreet table I can see. It's a booth in the corner—the table hidden from the large windows down the side of the coffee shop.

My jaw tics as I try and maintain my cool, watching the entrance to the cafe like a hawk.

I have no doubt what this is about.

Zoe knew that we weren't a long-term thing—hell, we weren't even a short-term thing. I haven't exchanged numbers with anyone in a long time, but there was a connection there. Even if we'd only intended for it to be a one-night stand.

And even though I can guess what's coming, I still catch my breath when Zoe appears in the doorway. She's so effortlessly beautiful, even dressed down in jeans and a T-shirt, her clutch slung over her arm. Her gaze scans the cafe, and as soon as her eyes meet mine, she gives a slight nod and walks toward my table. She's not timid in her approach, and by the time those long legs wrapped in denim make their way to me, I'm hard as a rock.

"Zoe. It's good to see you."

She smiles, but it doesn't meet her eyes. I've seen enough smiles like that to know it's for show. My stomach sinks as it becomes clear she wants to meet in public for a reason. My suspicion's confirmed.

"You too. Thank you for coming." Zoe sinks into the seat opposite. She chews her bottom lip, and it's endearing. It brings a smirk to my face to think of how good it felt to have those luscious lips wrapped around my cock. She was beautiful that night, but sitting here all fresh-faced and looking innocent, she's gorgeous.

I'd never seriously planned for it, but would she be up for round two?

"I remembered how you took your coffee in Vegas. White, one sugar."

She nods. "Thank you."

"You're welcome."

Just as she sits, the waitress approaches and delivers the coffee.

Zoe flashes her a smile, and I nod.

"Thank you," I say as she places the cups in front of us.

Zoe waits a moment, fisting her hands and flexing them. "There's no easy way to say this, so I'm just going to come out with it." Her brows knit as she gazes at me. "I'm pregnant."

Shit.

Here we go. Again.

The thing that comes with fame is that people will come out of the woodwork from all over the place to make claims on you. I'm not sure why, but I'd thought she was different. "Okay."

"You're the only guy I've slept with in the past six months, so ..." She scratches her nails against the tablecloth, and it's all kinds of distracting.

"What is it you're after, Zoe? Money? I'm not interested in a family. And I'll want a DNA test."

Her eyes widen. "I think you misunderstand. I'm not asking you for anything. I don't need it. I thought I should tell you because the last thing I need is some shitty tabloid somehow finding out the paternity of my baby and catching you by surprise."

I think my dick shrivels up and dies. "Oh."

She gives me a strained smile. "I mean, I'll add you to the birth certificate if you want, and I'd never deny you being a part of your child's life. But I'm not here for anything—I just wanted you to know."

My heart's in my throat. This isn't how I'd thought this conversation would go at all.

Zoe picks up her coffee and takes a sip, closing her eyes and letting out a moan that would make the dead stand up and take notice. It ripples through my body and my cock, which was trying to hide after she told me she didn't need me, is paying attention.

For years, I never wanted commitment.

Now I'm not wanted, I want more.

What fresh hell is this?

"This is good coffee."

I blink twice and give my head a little shake to wake myself out of the trance I seem to be in. "Oh. Yes. I love this place." *I've never been here before.*

Her lips curve into a smile. It's a lot warmer this time. "I can see why."

My head spins. I'm not sure what just happened. And I'm not sure I like it. Isn't this what I always wanted—to be free of any responsibility? I've walked away from my career, and that was the last thing left.

Zoe's having my baby, and she's happy for me to walk away too.

The thought of that sits heavy in my gut.

I've been sitting with her for maybe five minutes, and my whole world has been turned upside down, and not for the reasons I'd thought.

I need to make conversation—need her to stay talking with me so I can figure this out in my head. "So, what is it you do?"

Zoe's eyebrows rise. "It's a long story."

"We can order more coffee."

She chuckles and shakes her head. "I think I'll just have this one, but I'm open to a juice or something afterward. I'm trying to cut back on caffeine."

I lean forward. "The baby?"

Zoe nods and shrugs. "I don't know if I can give it up completely, but I can be a bit of a coffee fiend, and that has to slow down. Thankfully, this coming year is a lot less stressful than the past few have been, so that shouldn't be hard."

"Why so?"

She bites her bottom lip. It's not fair. I've spent the past few weeks thinking about this woman—talking myself out of contacting her—and now she's here and making me hard all over again.

"The short version is that I work in tech. I created a dating app which I sold a couple of years ago and now I'm working out the rest of my contract with the company. The more they integrate it into their system, the less I have to do."

I cock my head. "Really?"

Her lips curl into a bemused smile. "You seem surprised."

Shrugging, I take a sip of coffee. "It's just not a story I'd imagine anyone hears often. That's brilliant."

"Thank you. I thought at the end of the year I'd need to work out what to do with the rest of my life. Looks like the universe decided." She lets out a sigh. "I'm not sure what's coming, but I hope you know that the baby will be well looked after."

My throat tightens. This is the weirdest conversation I think I've ever had. While this isn't the first time I've dealt with the pregnancy talk, this is the first time I'm being left out of it.

I'm not sure I like it.

What the hell is happening to me?

"Zoe. I ..." What do I want? Do I want to take responsibility? Do I want her? I mean, I'd take her home in a heartbeat—

if anything, seeing her dressed casually without a lick of makeup and her hair scraped back, is even better than the night we met.

She looks like ... her.

Her blue eyes sparkle, and she tilts her head forward as if she's waiting for me to continue.

"This is a lot to take in," I finally continue. "I need a little time to process it and what it means."

Zoe's lips curl into a smile. "I can understand. It took me by surprise. I know we were careful."

I nod.

She rises from the table. "Thank you for the coffee. You've got my number. Call me if you want to talk."

Her hips sway as she swishes away, and I can't take my eyes off her ass.

I'm not immune to her in any way, shape, or form.

What the hell do I do?

SEVEN
DECLAN

THE NEXT FEW days are torture.

I keep on avoiding Nikki's calls and wallow in melancholy—not that I'm really sure why. I've ended my career on my terms. My life is going exactly how I want it to go.

Except for one thing.

Zoe's on my mind.

I had fun with her that night. It was more than just the sex, although that was spectacular. And now she's carrying my child—a child she's happy to have with no ties to me.

That doesn't sit well with me.

I still want her.

The one thing I've never had in all these years is family. Mom and Dad disowned me years ago for my bad behaviour, and my sister sided with them after I divorced my first wife. I can't blame any of them for that, but being alone sent me into an even bigger spiral and a second misguided marriage.

I should be elated that Zoe wants to do this without me. Instead, I'm floating on a sea of uncertainty, unsure why I'm not relieved.

Despite my two marriages, I never wanted children. I'd discussed it with my first wife, but we'd both decided to wait until we were older with our careers more established. When my career took off, I quickly went off the rails, and we weren't married much longer.

My second wife was a party girl who I married on a drunken whim. She would never have stood still long enough to have children, and I had no interest by then.

And now there's Zoe. Zoe, who blew my mind with the one night we spent together. Zoe, who has the world at her feet.

Zoe, who didn't even need to tell me she was pregnant.

The first thing I did when I came home from the coffee house was to search for Zoe on the Internet. It didn't take long to find her.

She created a dating app with built-in safety check-ins. Women adored it, and it had taken off fast. So much so that a bidding war erupted before she settled for the company she felt was the best fit. It's weird—I barely know her, but a sense of pride creeps over me as I read the stories about her.

She's now working in San Francisco with the company that bought her app while they integrate it into their systems. Whatever that means.

Her app sold for so much that unless she eats Ferraris for breakfast, she'll never have to worry about money ever again.

An ache sits in the pit of my stomach at the thought that

she doesn't need me. I'm used to being the breadwinner in the relationship, but compared to Zoe, I'm a pauper.

I have nothing to offer her.

For the first time in years I'm unsettled. I've always been so confident, but this has shaken me to the core.

If this had happened with nearly any other woman, I'd be able to offer to support her, but Zoe doesn't need it. She's made that very clear.

But I still want to.

I want to. I want this.

I want her.

It's not just her, though. I'm going to be a father. She sounded like she was open to my involvement, but to what extent?

Maybe I start by reaching out to tell her I want to be involved. I want to see her belly grow with my baby, and be there to pamper her when she needs a pick-me-up.

I've made up my mind about my career—I could even move to be close to her.

Before I can talk myself out of it, I pick up the phone and click on her contact.

"Hello?" Her voice is thick with sleep, and I do a double take at the time. But it's after ten in the morning—pretty early for me.

"Zoe, it's Declan."

She clears her throat. "I know. I have caller ID. Are you okay? Why are you calling?"

"Are you still in bed?" I don't know why I ask—no, I do know. I want to be there with her.

"No, I made it as far as the couch this morning before feeling gross, and then I fell asleep."

I swallow hard. There's some vague memory from friends' pregnancies that it's not much fun in the early days. Probably not later on either.

Frowning, I scan my memory. Is pregnancy *any* fun at all?

"I'm sorry to hear that. I was wondering if I could come and see you. I'll fly up. We need to talk."

She sighs. "That sounds heavy."

"Nothing too crazy, I promise."

"Sure." She sounds exhausted. "I'll text you my address because I doubt I'm leaving this couch any time soon."

I chuckle. "Sure. Do you need me to bring anything? I'll get there later this afternoon."

"No, thanks. I've got the couch and the TV, and that's all I need for the moment."

"I'll see you soon. If I can get a flight."

Her laughter warms my heart. "You haven't even booked anything?"

"No, I wanted to make sure you were okay with me turning up first."

"That's very thoughtful of you."

I grin. Anything I can do to get points with her is a bonus. "Send me that address and I'll keep in touch."

As soon as we've disconnected the call, I dial my assistant. Most of the time he gets paid for doing nothing—I've never really seen the need for him, but my manager insisted. But he is useful for when I need to sort things out at the last moment.

"Declan?" He crunches in my ear.

"You answered the phone while eating?" I roll my eyes.

Joel's quiet for a moment. If I had to guess, I'd say he's swallowing his food. "I knew it was you."

"I love how you just don't care." I laugh.

"You're the best boss I've ever had. You leave me alone."

I shake my head. "I need you to get a flight for me. LA to San Fran."

"What date?"

"Today."

He sighs. "Let me see what I can do."

"I know it's last minute, but I really need to get there this afternoon. Organise a rental car while you're at it."

"Sure thing, boss. I'll call you back."

Lord knows Joel doesn't have a lot to do, but I can trust him to step up when I need him to. Within thirty minutes, he has a plane ticket and rental car details in my inbox, and I order a taxi to get me to the airport.

When I need to be driven around, I hire someone but usually, I chauffeur myself. I've never been freer.

And with my retirement, this is just the start. I've been in the public eye since I was fifteen years old, so the idea of having no attention on me appeals more than it maybe should.

It's not a long flight, and Joel's managed to get me an economy seat, but I'm grateful that he got me any seat at all, so I don't complain. But I am glad when I can get off the plane and stretch my legs.

I bring up the address Zoe sent me on Google Maps and use the GPS to get there in the rental car.

After finding a place to park, I head straight up to her apartment, and ring the doorbell.

The door opens, and my breath hitches.

Even dressed down in sweats with her hair piled up into a messy bun, Zoe is breathtakingly beautiful.

"Declan. Come in." She turns and I follow her into the apartment, closing the door behind me.

Her apartment is spacious. The living room is big and laid out for comfort. There's a couch and two recliners, and she has a few beanbags scattered around.

When we reach the couch, she drops down onto it with a sigh, and I take a seat beside her.

"How are you feeling?" I ask.

She shrugs. "Better than earlier. I need to get a handle on this whole morning sickness, but whoever named it is a liar. It lasted nearly all day."

"I'm sorry to hear that."

Her lips twitch. "You should be. It's your fault I'm in this situation."

My mouth falls open, my palm to my chest. "Me? It takes two to tango, lady."

Zoe laughs, and it's almost musical. "You got me there. I'm still blaming you, though."

"I'm glad we can talk like this."

Her cheeks dimple when she smiles. "Me too." She draws in a deep breath. "I was a little scared about telling you. But my conscience wouldn't let me not do it. You should know if there's a mini you out there."

A mini me. My chest tightens.

"I ... I'm glad you called me. I'm in this weird place in my life right now, and I realised that maybe this is something I need."

Her eyebrows shoot up. I'm fumbling this all of a sudden.

"I mean, yes it's unexpected, but I don't know if it's a bad thing. And clearly you want to go through with it."

She nods. "Why are you here, Declan? What do you want?"

"I want in."

Her eyes search mine. "What do you mean?"

"I want to be a part of my kid's life. Whatever you'll give me."

Zoe frowns. "I have to say I'm surprised."

"You're not the only one."

She runs her gaze over my face before she meets mine again. "What does that mean?"

Reaching for her hand, I run my fingers down hers before I give them a squeeze. "I can't stop thinking about us raising our child together. I want to try."

Her rapid blinking tells me I've really caught her unawares. This isn't what she was expecting. But am I really surprised? I've reacted to this in a way I never saw coming either.

"I was thinking maybe we could spend time together?"

One of her eyebrows arches and she pulls her hand back.

Holding up my palms, I lean back. "Platonically. I'm not expecting us to just jump into a relationship—we don't really know each other. But ..."

"I don't know."

I blow out a long breath. "It's just ... all these years, I never thought I'd be a father. When I wasn't working, I was partying. And now I'm at the end of my career, and this is my chance."

She chews on her bottom lip.

"There's so much I want to experience, and I didn't realise how much I wanted this until you ... until you told me you were pregnant." I lean forward. "I want to be there for you through this pregnancy. I want to be there for the scans. Maybe even be there when the baby's born? But clearly I can't do it without your agreement."

Setting her jaw, she crosses her arms and seems to consider me. "I guess you could push the issue legally."

"Maybe. I haven't looked into it. I'd rather keep this amicable and work with you on it. I know—I know you said you don't need anything from me, but I want to offer you my full support through this. No one should go through it alone."

She hesitates. "I'll consider it."

"That's all I'll ask."

She's a smart woman. She knows that I could work through my lawyer, but I don't want that. I don't want this to turn into some kind of legal transaction. I've had paternity claims before, but this is different. She literally wants nothing from me.

I'm not sure I have much to offer.

I'm a hollow wreck of a man who has been on a slide for a very long time.

Maybe it's selfish, but I think this could make me feel whole again.

"I'll go and find a hotel room nearby, and give you some time to think about it."

She shakes her head. "I'm not sure how long I'll need. Maybe it'd be better for you to go home."

"I've got nothing but time right now, sweetheart. I'll stay close if that's okay."

She nods, and I cheer inside.

I'd much rather be near for her, and even this concession feels like a win.

EIGHT
ZOE

I'M NOT sure what to do.

I'd resigned myself to bringing up my baby alone, and now Declan has thrown a spanner in the works.

A very good-looking, sexy spanner, but a spanner nonetheless.

I don't have an issue with him wanting to be a part of the baby's life, but realistically, is this going to stick? Will we just be a novelty and disposable, or is he going to commit to eighteen years of co-parenting?

If only I knew him well enough to work that out.

I guess if this is a novelty to him, he'll lose interest before the baby's old enough to miss him.

Maybe.

It's so hard to know what to do.

When he didn't call me, and then when he was taken aback by my lack of demands, I'd thought that was the last I'd see of him.

His interest in the baby has caught me by surprise.

It scares me a little. He has the ability to really mess with me if things go bad. I might have the money for lawyers, but so does he. And the last thing I need is any kind of custody battle. It was hard enough thinking about what I needed to do when my contract finished, let alone the added complication of my baby-daddy wanting to be involved.

Although the thought of spending more time with Declan intrigues me.

When he didn't contact me after Las Vegas, I'd thought it was pretty clear that he didn't want anything more with me, and maybe he still doesn't. But I'm still as drawn to him now as I was that night, and if the chemistry between us is still the same, who knows what will happen?

If things were different, then maybe I might think that we could form a relationship out of this—some kind of mutual understanding based on being parents. But I know his reputation and even though he talked about making a fresh start and retiring from acting, how easy would it be for him to slip back into old habits?

It'll be hard to resist him if we see each other often.

I need to keep my wits about me. But I also can't find a way to justify not including him when he wants to be involved in this pregnancy.

My phone buzzes.

Caitlin: *Can I video call you? I feel like we need to catch up.*

Me: *I would love that. I need to talk.*

I go to my desk and open my laptop. Within seconds, I've

got a call request coming through, and I breathe a sigh of relief as Caitlin comes into focus. She's my person.

"Hey," she says. "Are you okay?"

"Declan's here."

Her mouth falls open. "Where? At your apartment?"

"Not now, but he was."

Her brows knit. "What's going on, Zoe? Do we need to find a lawyer? What does he want?"

"He wants to be a part of his child's life. He's suggesting we spend time together so he can share the pregnancy with me."

"Oh my god." She gapes at me.

"What's going on?" Brandon's voice echoes in the background. "Is that Zoe? Is she okay? Do I have to kick someone's ass?"

I laugh. Even though they're more than two thousand miles away, they're still protective of me.

"She's fine, but Declan wants to be there for her and the baby." Caitlin claps her hands like a performing seal.

"Baby? What baby?"

I freeze. Caitlin's so bad at keeping secrets when it comes to Brandon. I guess this one is no exception.

"Zoe's pregnant," she says.

Brandon sticks his face in front of the computer screen, and for a moment, all I can see is a stray nose hair. I laugh again and shake my head.

"Really? Do I say congrats?" A tentative smile is on his lips.

Caitlin shoves him out of the way. "Yes. Zoe's happy. But she thought she was doing it alone."

His eyebrow twitches. "Alone? You're never alone, babe. Play your cards right and you can move here. I can start a harem."

Caitlin rolls her eyes. "I read a book last week that featured one. Now he won't shut up about it."

I blow her a kiss. "I miss you guys."

"We miss you. What are you going to do about Declan?" She turns to Brandon. "Zoe told him she didn't need him, but he wants to be involved."

I shrug. "This isn't what I expected, but I'm going to think about it. He's staying nearby for a while, and I'll give him the answer when I'm ready."

Brandon strokes his beard. "I think you should give the guy a chance. You gave him an out, but he's not taking it."

"I just worry that he won't stick to it. If it's during the pregnancy it only affects me, but once the baby's here ..."

"Yeah, but how are you going to know if you don't try? You know you've always got us. Even if you've got that weird accent."

I laugh. Brandon always teases me about my New Zealand accent. "Thanks. I know I can always rely on you."

Caitlin snuggles against him, and it hits me right in the gut. *I want that.* I want a love of my own. Have I screwed this up by getting pregnant to Declan?

"Anyway, I'm going to get going. I have a lot of thinking to do, and I'm ready to get some sleep. Love you guys." I blow them more kisses before we disconnect the video call.

Can I do this? Can I trust him to stay involved?

My biggest fear would be that he just up and leaves one day when my child is old enough to know who he is. I could deal with any financial fallout—it's the emotional fallout I'm worried about.

On the other hand, Brandon is right. Declan had an out. I told him I wanted nothing. And yet he wants to be involved.

Maybe I need to take a leap of faith.

AFTER SLEEPING ON IT, I send a text to Declan in the morning.

Me: Can you come over? We need to talk.

Declan: Be there in ten.

Twenty minutes later, a knock on the door breaks me out of my thoughts.

He hustles in the door, coffee cups in one hand, paper bags in the other.

"Sorry I'm a little late. I stopped to get some breakfast, and I thought you might like something too."

My stomach grumbles. "That sounds great. My morning sickness is so up and down. One minute I want to hurl, the next I'm ravenous."

He leans over and pecks me on the cheek. His kiss burns on my skin. "I didn't know what you'd feel like, so there's a selection."

I follow him to the coffee table where he places everything, and join him on the couch.

"I wasn't sure if you were drinking coffee still, so I got you a coffee and a hot chocolate. Hope that's okay."

My stomach makes a gurgling sound, and I laugh. "That's more than okay."

Leaning over, he tears open the bags to reveal different pastries before holding out his palm and pointing toward them. "Lady's choice."

Grinning, I reach for a big, fat pastry stuffed with chocolate. I close my eyes and bite into the sweet treat. The chocolate inside explodes in my mouth, and I let out a moan.

"Jesus, Zoe. What are you trying to do to me?"

I open my eyes. Declan's gaze is firmly fixed on my lips.

"I'm sorry?"

"I still have a lot of thoughts about our night together. I'm not going to pretend that you moaning doesn't ... do things to me."

"Me?" I place a hand on my heart. "Little old me who you didn't call after our Vegas sex-a-thon."

He drops his gaze to the floor. "We need to talk about that."

"Maybe. But what we really need to talk about is your involvement with our baby."

His eyes flicker up to meet mine. "Our baby."

"We did make it together." I smile. "I thought about what you asked, and I'm happy for you to be included."

He presses his palms together. "Thank you."

I bite my lip. "But if you're going to be involved, then I don't want any fly-by-night. I'm not looking for you to commit to me, but you do have to commit to this baby."

He's quiet for a moment. "I understand, and I'm ready for this. I'm so ready. I'll move closer to you. I'm retiring from acting, and I'd rather be close so I can be there for appointments and when the baby arrives."

My throat tightens. "Really?"

He chuckles. "Yes, Zoe. I want to be there for you and this baby. I'll find an apartment down the road."

"Why don't you stay with me?" The words are out before I can stop them. *What am I doing?*

We fall into an uneasy silence. But really, it does make sense. I have plenty of room and he wants to be involved in both the pregnancy and the baby's life.

"I mean, if you want to." I fumble the words but get them out. "We can revisit it after the baby's born. I was already planning on making a decision about whether to stay here or go home to New Zealand about then anyway."

"You ... you're thinking about leaving?"

I close my eyes. "I was. My visa won't last forever, and there's nothing left for me here ... was nothing left for me here."

"You don't have to make a decision yet."

"I sigh. "Everything feels so complicated."

He pauses. "Maybe. But it's only as complicated as we make it. It'll be easier when I'm there and we can talk it out. Make plans."

I nod. "That sounds okay."

"Are you really alright with me moving in?"

Pausing, I nod again. "It makes sense. My friend Caitlin used to live across the hall and I had her nearby to help, but now she's moved away and it's just me."

"There's no time like the present."

"So soon? You don't have to rush."

His warm hand covers mine. "You're not alone. I'll be here for you. Give me a few days to go home and sort some things and then I'll be back."

My heart thuds—I'm not sure it's safe while he's around. My attraction to him is there and as strong as it was that first night.

And from the look in his eyes, I don't think it's one-sided.

NINE
ZOE

ALL MORNING I've been unsure if I have morning sickness or just butterflies over Declan moving in.

We know nothing about each other.

It's weird. When I first told him about the baby, I was sure he was going to run a mile. The way he assumed that I was after his money or whatever had made me mad, but this turnaround has me second guessing everything.

He's been gone a week, and although he's kept in touch, the idea of him being here all the time makes my stomach twist.

My room has an en-suite, so we have a fair bit of private space, but we'll still be sharing the rest of the apartment.

I have yet to tell my parents what's happening.

They don't even know I'm pregnant.

But I shove all that aside when there's a knock on the door and I have no doubt about who's on the other side.

I take a deep breath and open the door.

He's so effortlessly handsome. In black jeans and a white collared shirt, he stands in my doorway and smiles. "Hi."

"Hi," I squeak, and his grin widens.

"It's okay, Zoe. I know this is weird."

I take a step back. "It is. Come in."

This isn't the first time he's been here, but this time he's looking around as if he's never seen the place. I guess there wasn't much reason to take in the scenery before.

I lead him down the hallway toward his room.

"Your apartment's even bigger than I'd thought."

That's it. That's all he says.

I bought a two-bedroom apartment because I liked having the extra space, and I figured I could always get a roommate if I wanted company.

And now I'm glad I've got the extra space for Declan.

"Thanks." I lead him into the spare room. "This is your room."

"We're not sharing?" He smirks, and I roll my eyes as he drops his suitcase on the bed. His laughter makes me smile. "I'm pulling your leg. I have no expectations. I'm just glad you're going to let me into my child's life."

"I'm still surprised you want to be a part of it."

He frowns, but then huffs out a breath and shrugs. "If I'm honest with myself, *I'm* surprised. A few years ago, things might have been different, but ..."

My eyebrows rise. "But?"

He places his hands on my shoulders. "I've just reached a point in my life where I need a fresh start. I like you, Zoe. And the idea of becoming a father doesn't scare me as much as it would have done in the past."

I cock my head. "But your first reaction ..."

"Old habits. I've dealt with pregnancy claims before, and none of them were mine."

"And you think mine is?"

He drops his hands. "I messed up when you told me. But I've been down this track before. No one's ever told me they don't need me though. They've never told me just out of courtesy. It's always been about money or fame. You're the real deal."

I swallow hard. "We can always do a paternity test if it makes you feel better. After the baby's born."

"Let's see what the next few months bring and cross that bridge when we get there." His smile is reassuring, which is weirdly what I need. He has the ability to do so much damage to me. If he takes me to court for custody, I don't know what would happen.

I'm lucky I can afford good lawyers, but I want us to at least be friendly, and that can't happen if there's a court battle.

For now, I tuck that to the back of my mind. Lucky it's easy to keep the peace with Declan. I wouldn't want to deal with the fallout if we disagreed.

"I'll ... I'll leave you to unpack and settle in. I've got an en suite attached to my room, so the main bathroom is all yours."

Before he says anything else, I turn and head down the hall. There are a million thoughts jostling for position in my head, and not all of them are positive. But having Declan here is good. It's better my baby has a father interested in their well-being than an absentee one.

He leaves me unsettled. I'm not sure I can ever get used

to that calm presence he projects. I don't even know this guy. What am I doing inviting him to live with me?

"I'll cook dinner," he calls out as he walks into the living room behind me.

"I ..." I'm not sure what I expected, but it wasn't that.

He chuckles. "Bet you thought I couldn't cook."

I shake my head. "I hadn't really thought about it at all."

"I've been looking after myself for years. Go and put your feet up. I've got this."

For a moment, I just stare at him.

"Zoe." He places his hands on my shoulders. "Let me take care of you."

"This wasn't part of the deal."

He shrugs. "There weren't really any specifics discussed. It makes sense to me. If you're okay, the baby's okay."

I blink rapidly, unable to process any thoughts.

"Go," he says gently.

"But—"

"We still need to talk about rent, but in the meantime, I've got to pay my way somehow." He plants a kiss on my forehead. What's with that? I'm a goner for forehead kisses. They cross any wall I try and put up.

He's being sweet.

It's not fair.

By the time I open my mouth again, he's already in the kitchen, opening cupboards and pulling out ingredients.

With a shake of my head, I make my way to the couch and pick up the remote control, turning on the television and scrolling through channels.

"Do you have any allergies?" he calls out.

I press more buttons on the remote. "No."

"Good. I know these are your groceries, but if I go shopping, then I know I can get anything."

My throat tightens. I get that he wants to be involved with the baby, but this is a lot. He's been here five minutes, and I'm already feeling pampered. I'm not sure I want this to stop.

"Zoe? You okay?" He pokes his head around the door and smiles.

"I'm fine. It's just ... this isn't how I imagined all of this." I wave my arms around.

His grin brings out dimples in his cheeks. "I want to be all in."

"What does that mean?"

He crosses the room and drops to his knees in front of me. "I mean, all of this. We might not be together, but it's making me happy to do what I can to make your life easier. You have enough on your plate with the baby and working out your contract."

"I didn't know that meant the whole domestication thing."

Declan chuckles. "I'm not sure how to describe this, but I feel more alive than I have in years. Like I'm really working toward something worthwhile here. A healthy, happy baby with a beautiful woman who I know is going to be an amazing mother."

I frown. "Don't you make me cry."

He pushes himself up until he's standing. "Only happy tears. I promise."

"Who are you?"

Cocking his head, his gaze burns through me. "I'm the father of that baby, and I'm not taking my responsibilities lightly."

For a moment, I can't drop my gaze from his.

"Relax and enjoy it." He winks before turning on his heel and heading back into the kitchen.

What the hell is going on?

TEN
ZOE

I'M STILL in a daze the following morning.

After a wonderful meal of garlic and herb chicken with the creamiest mashed potato I think I've ever eaten, Declan washed the dishes and then retreated to his room to watch television.

I slept better than I have done in ages.

Scrubbing my face with my hands, I head into the kitchen to make some coffee to start the day.

I'm going into work this afternoon to talk to Jason and Chrissie—the owners of the company who bought my app. As I'm partway through the final year of my contract, and this is the year things ease up, I'm hoping they'll be receptive to the time I'm going to need to take off.

I close my eyes as the coffee machine does its thing, and breathe in the aroma of a freshly made brew before pouring a cup and turning to leave the room.

"Good morning."

Crash.

The cup shatters when it hits the tiled floor, spraying hot coffee everywhere. A few drops splash on my legs, and they sting but only for an instant.

I shriek, and stand completely still, surveying the damage.

"Oh shit. I'm sorry. I didn't mean to give you a fright."

I hold up my palms. "It's okay. It's my fault. I forgot you were here."

My racing heart slows and I raise my gaze to take in the sight of Declan standing in my kitchen. He's shirtless, his pyjama pants sitting low on his hips.

That's not fair.

Why does he look so gorgeous in the morning, and I probably resemble a cat dragged through a hedge backward?

"I'll clean up, Zoe, and make you a fresh cup?" His eyes dart around the room. "Stay there a second. Do you have a mop?"

"In the hall cupboard."

He reappears moments later and brushes the shattered pieces of mug out of my way so I can leave the kitchen. "Go and sit in the living room. I'll bring you a coffee when I'm done."

I gingerly make my way across the cold floor and into the living room before dropping onto the couch.

What an idiot.

Where was my brain this morning? I woke up feeling pretty good considering the past week I've had morning sickness and been barely able to stomach breakfast. But my mind must have been on another planet to have forgotten Declan's presence in my home.

He's not really forgettable.

I'm so lost in thought that I jump again when he brushes my cheek with his thumb.

"You're so cute when you're flustered."

I glower at him but take the mug he's holding out for me. Cute? I'm mad at myself for what just happened. Who forgets when they have Declan O'Leary in their spare room?

Is this baby brain?

I frown.

"Hey, it's not that bad."

He drops onto the couch beside me and places his cup on the coffee table. Extending his arm, he reaches out and pushes a stray lock of hair behind my ear.

I force a smile. "I'm sorry. I was away with the fairies. Truth be told, I forgot you were here."

Declan chuckles. "You've lived by yourself for a while, I assume. It takes time to get used to living with people again."

He caresses my cheek before dropping his hand, and I close my eyes briefly as I miss his touch. There's no denying he still has an effect on me.

I will not crush on him.

I can't.

He's here for the baby—not for me. I have to remember that.

"Your foot's bleeding."

I look down. It's only a drop of blood, but I wince when he plucks a sliver of mug out that I didn't even realise was there.

"Got it. Where's your first-aid kit?"

I swallow hard. "Um, bathroom cabinet."

"Stay here. I'll be back in an instant." He gives my knee a reassuring squeeze and I blow out a breath as he goes to the bathroom and returns with a plastic box.

His gentle hands caress my foot, and he slips the Band-Aid over my cut before running his hand up to my ankle and placing my foot back on the ground. "I know you're going out this afternoon, but rest it."

"It's just a tiny cut."

"Maybe, but it's my fault."

I shake my head. "No. I hadn't had coffee at the time. Caffeine's what I need to wake myself up."

"Well, for future reference the coffee goes inside you, not on the floor."

I slap his bicep. "Be quiet, you."

Declan grins. "Living with you is going to be fun."

"I'm not sure about that. Wait until I'm bloated and angry at the world."

He chuckles. "You'll still be adorable."

How can I argue with that?

I DRAW in a deep breath as I approach the boardroom.

I'm in the office less and less as my contract comes to a close, but I don't want to presume that Jason and Chrissie will be okay with the amount of time off that I'll need—even if my pregnancy goes okay.

They're waiting for me when I enter the room and slip into a chair next to Chrissie.

Her brows are knit—I haven't told them what this is about

and she's probably concerned as I've not called them together for a meeting since the sale was done and dusted. I haven't had to. This integration has gone so well, we've only really had our scheduled project meetings and haven't had to get together over anything else.

"I'm sure you two are wondering why I wanted to meet with you." I hold up my palms. "It's nothing bad, but in the interests of the open and honest working relationship I have with you, I wanted you to know I'm pregnant."

Chrissie's mouth falls open. "I didn't think that was what was about to come out of your mouth. Are you ... happy?"

I sigh. "Well, it's taken a bit of getting used to because I didn't plan on it happening. I'd like to say it won't affect my work until the baby's born, but I think we all know that's not true. For now, things are good, but I'm not really sure what the future holds."

"Can I just say something?" Jason leans on the table, knitting his fingers together.

I nod.

"It's okay, Zoe. Most of the handover is done, and we knew there wouldn't be three years' worth of full-time work." He smiles.

I breathe out a sigh of relief. I lucked out with the deal I took. It wasn't the most money, but it was with a company that seemed ethically aligned with my own beliefs, and the reason why I created the app in the first place.

"Besides, you've done far more than we'd ever thought." Chrissie picks up the conversation. "Instead of just consulting, you've played an active role in integrating your app into our servers, and honestly, you can just put your feet up and coast the rest of the year. Not that I'd imagine you'll get to do much of that, being pregnant."

I sniff. "You're so good to me."

"You've increased the value of our company by so much more than we ever imagined. The site is doing well, and our reputation out there for client safety is second to none. We'll keep you on the project emails, and if you want to, you can dial into the meetings, but no stress." Chrissie grasps my arm. "I've got two of my own, so I know how demanding pregnancy can be."

"Thank you. I didn't know how well this would go down, and..."

"It happens. We knew we were a good match when we did the deal, and you could have not said anything, but I'm glad you did."

I leave the office with a spring in my step. It's like everything is falling into place.

My pregnancy might have been unplanned, but it seems to have come at a good time in my life. Whatever happens with Declan, I'll be there for my child no matter what, and I can provide for them.

My mouth waters as I step into my apartment, and the aroma of tomato floats through the air. I'm not sure what he's cooking, but Declan stands at the stovetop, stirring something in a pan.

"Honey, I'm home." I laugh at my own joke before shaking my head.

He turns, his eyes glistening with amusement. "Good day?"

I draw in a deep breath while walking toward the

breakfast bar. "Yeah, it was. I'm just going to ride through the rest of my contract. If they need me, they'll let me know."

He grins. "Great. I'm making my world-famous spaghetti bolognaise."

I laugh. "World famous?"

"Well, in my own house. But I'll share with you." He winks, and I let out a little sigh before catching myself.

"I should think so." I lean my elbows on the bench. "Seeing as I'm carrying your heir."

Declan snorts with laughter, and I join in, loving the sound.

I thought at least in these early days we'd be tiptoeing around each other, but it's almost like we're a couple already.

Already?

That might never happen.

And that's beginning to be a depressing thought.

"I need to call my parents. They don't know I'm pregnant yet." Today seems as good a day as any given how well it's going.

"Want me to sit in on the call?"

My eyes widen. "You'd do that?"

"In this together. Remember?"

I blow out a breath. "As grateful as I am, I think I need to do this alone. Maybe introduce you later?"

He shrugs. "Whatever you think. As long as you know I'm here for you."

"I think you've shown that already."

"Go and make your call. I'll have dinner ready when you're finished."

I pat the bench. "You're so good to me." He gives me a pleased smile before I walk away.

After grabbing my laptop from my desk in the living room, I carry it into the bedroom and close the door behind me.

My parents will be at home—it's around three p.m. on Sunday afternoon there. This is the time I would usually call them. I haven't spoken to them in a couple of weeks, which isn't unheard of but also isn't like me, so they'll probably already know there's something up.

I take a deep breath and hit the call button.

It takes a few moments, but my mother's face soon fills up the screen and she beams a smile at me.

"Zoe. I wondered if you'd call today. It's so good to see your face."

"You too. Is Dad around?"

Her brows twitch. "Sure."

"I wanted to talk to you both."

She smiles. "I'll go and get your father."

Video calling was something I had to teach my parents about when I left New Zealand and talking on the phone wasn't enough. Mum often had to lay eyes on me to make sure I was okay in that first year, and Dad can be a bit overprotective with me being their only child.

"Hey, sweetheart." Dad smiles as he appears on the screen. Mum joins him a moment later. "You okay?"

Might as well dive on in.

"I'm pregnant."

Both of them stare at me as if I have two heads. Of course they know I have sex—I'm thirty. I've had relationships both short and long, but nothing that ever got close to me having a baby with someone.

"I didn't know you were dating," Mum says.

I bite my bottom lip. "Well, the thing is, that I'm not."

They exchange a glance, and I roll my eyes.

"Are you okay with this?" Dad says. "Do you need to come home?"

I fight a smile. He asks me this every time we talk no matter how good or mundane the news is I have for them. Deep down, he just wants me back under his roof.

"No, I'm fine. I've still got to the end of my contract to work through. Besides, this year the workload is winding down, so I'll be working from home all the time."

He nods slowly.

"What about the father?" Mum asks. "Is he ... in the picture?"

Breathing out a long, slow breath, I choose my next words carefully. "He is. Actually, he just moved in with me yesterday because he wants to be there for us."

"Oh." Mum frowns. "So you are seeing him?"

I shake my head. "No, we're not together. But he wants to do right by the baby. I told him he didn't need to, but—"

"The man clearly has his head screwed on straight. Are we going to meet him?" Dad asks.

I shrug. "Maybe? I'm not sure when."

"This all sounds very weird." Mum and Dad exchange another glance, and I fist my hands.

"I had a one-night stand with him. That was all it was supposed to be. And I told him he didn't have to be there for us, and I could do it alone."

Mum gasps.

"There's something else I should tell you," I continue. "Eventually something will come out about it because of who he is. He's an actor—Declan O'Leary."

Dad's brows rise and Mum's eyes widen.

"He's a movie star?" she asks.

I nod. "He is."

"I'm sure I've read stories about him in the magazines. Is he really who you want as your baby's father?"

I roll my eyes again. "It's not like I chose this. It just ... happened. And Declan's a good guy. Like I said, I gave him an out, but he didn't take it."

Dad sets his jaw. God only knows what he's thinking. Declan's just ten years younger than my father—Declan's 45 to Dad's 55. They're closer in age than Declan and I am, and I'm sure the second we're off this call, he'll be searching for anything he can find on him.

"I usually trust your judgement, but are you sure?"

I nod. Even if I have doubts, I'm not about to admit them to my parents. Will Declan stay the course? I have no idea. Maybe if I knew him better I might be more confident, but I'm not and I'm not sure how a man who's led such a big life would be content playing house with me.

"We have to work this out for ourselves. I love you guys, and I wanted you to know that you're going to be grandparents, so please trust me to do what's right?"

Dad frowns and Mum nods. I'm not sure I can win this battle.

"So, uhh, other than that, work has been really good. My workload was going to be a lot lighter these next few months anyway, and at the end of the year I'll decide what I'm doing next. Although I'll have the baby by then and I'm sure I'll be busy with other things." I laugh, trying to lift the mood.

"I'm happy for you," Mum says. Dad stands and walks away, and I let out a sigh. "Give him some time, Zoe. He'll come around. Whatever happens, you know we're here for you."

"I know," I whisper. "I just wish he'd treat me like an adult."

"It's hard when your baby grows up." She smiles. "But you'll be a good mother, and I'm here whenever you need me, even if you have to call me at some ridiculous hour."

"Thanks, Mum."

"I'll go and check on him. Take care of yourself and please let me know if there's anything I can do. I love you."

"Love you too."

With the call disconnected, I sit and gather my thoughts. That could have gone better, but it could also have gone a lot worse. Dad's cautious—I know that. He's taken care of me more than once when my young heart's been broken.

But Declan and I aren't together.

This is different.

Isn't it?

ELEVEN
DECLAN

ZOE CLOSES her eyes and leans back in her chair, patting her still flat stomach with her hand. "You can cook that for me anytime."

"I will."

She opens her eyes and smiles. "Thank you, Declan. I don't know if I'll ever want you to move out again at this rate."

"Just as well I have no plans to." I shoot her a wink. That's becoming a habit. But she makes me want to flirt with her when I'd thought I was so dead inside.

"I wasn't sure what your plans would be ... after the baby's born."

"We'll work it out when we have to." I reach for her hand and give it a squeeze. "There's no rush. I'm here for the duration, and I'll cook this every night if it's what you feel like."

"I'm getting very spoiled."

I run my thumb over the back of her hand. "As you

should be." Tell me more about your day. You said you can just ride out your contract?"

She pulls her arm away and blows out a long breath. "Well, I told them I was pregnant. And they told me that they don't really need me."

"So, you're not working anymore?" I ask.

She nods slowly. "I've been doing a lot more than my contract requires, and it's meant that the integration has happened faster. This year was going to be a lot of sitting around and maybe offering support, but it looks like that's not even really needed. I'll still be logging in and sitting in on project meetings, but my role was always going to be downgraded this year."

"Our timing was pretty good, then."

Her mouth falls open. "I'm not sure if I'd say that."

"Just in terms of your contract. And my retirement. It's all working out well."

I'm not even sure what I'm saying. But I do know that Zoe's pregnancy is already helping keep me grounded. I'm not remotely tempted to drink, and if I spend tonight in front of the television instead of out on the town, it wouldn't be a hardship.

My only doubt is around whether I could keep that up or not.

Will this always be enough? Or will I go back to wanting more?

I can't think that way.

"I guess you could say we're going okay." She shrugs. "I always thought I'd be settled down before I had babies, but I also thought it'd be before I hit thirty."

"Thirty isn't old to have a baby."

"No, but my life just didn't work out the way I'd thought it would." She smiles. "Mind you, I also didn't anticipate creating Date Me and the deal to sell it." Her eyes meet mine. "If things don't work, Declan, and you want to go back to your life, you know we'll be okay, right?"

"I do know that, but I have no intention of going anywhere."

KNOWING we'll be in each other's pockets leaves me restless. We've gone from a one-night stand to not only living together, but being at home together all the time.

Is that really a good way to get to know someone?

The first night I was here, I slept well knowing that Zoe and the baby were safe under the same roof as me. The second night, I toss and turn, wondering how quickly she'll get sick of me being under her feet.

When daylight peeps through the curtains, I give in and make my way to the kitchen to get started on breakfast.

Zoe's beaten me to it.

I breathe in the heady smell of coffee, and come to a stop when I reach the living room.

Oh dear God.

She exits the kitchen, dressed in a shirt and a pair of pink cotton panties.

Is she trying to kill me?

Sitting at her desk, she places her mug beside her laptop and opens the laptop lid.

It's far too late for my cock, which is already standing to attention. I shift my gaze to the floor.

The Band-Aid on her foot makes me wince.

Zoe looks up. "You okay?"

"I ... uhhh ... I was just reminded of yesterday. Is your foot sore?"

She shakes her head. "No, it's fine." Cracking a smile, she stands. "See? Good as gold. It was an accident, Declan. I'm all good."

"Doesn't make me feel less guilty."

She crosses the room and grips my arm. "Please don't. I just have to get used to living with someone again."

"Uhh, I can tell."

Her eyes widen, and she looks down at what she's wearing. She lifts her hand from my arm and slaps her palm across her mouth before letting out a loud giggle.

"Oh my god. I never wear pants when I'm working at home."

"I've seen you naked, but I'm not sure if I can cope with this every day."

One of her brows arches, and her gaze sweeps down to my groin.

Oh God, have mercy.

"That's not helping." The words leave my lips before I can help it. Is that going to upset her? Is she ever going to trust me if I'm walking around with a hard-on twenty-four hours a day?

"I'm sorry." Her voice is husky, which just makes it worse.

"I think I'm going to have to start every day with a cold

shower if you're prancing around in your underwear," I grumble.

She laughs again. "I wish I could say I was sorry, but it's good to know I still have that effect."

"Why would you not?" I hold out my palms. "You know I think you're beautiful."

Tilting her head, she smirks at me. "Because I'm pregnant. I know you want to be here for the baby, but that has to be so unattractive to a man who didn't want a baby to start with." She sighs. "I'll go and put some shorts on."

As she steps away, I reach out and grasp her arm. "That's not how I feel. You're still the most beautiful woman I've ever seen."

Zoe snorts. "I've seen your co-stars. I know that's not true."

"But it is. It's what drew me to you in the first place. And pregnancy doesn't make you less attractive." I tug her closer. "If anything, it makes you even more gorgeous. That's my baby you're carrying."

Her expression straightens out and she swallows hard.

"Declan." Her soft tone tells me I've hit the mark. And I meant it. I knew she was special the moment I laid eyes on her, and that's my child in there. All the years of boozing and women, and I got it right with the right mother of my child. I know it.

"I'm a lucky man, Zoe. Even if we're not together."

She fans her face with her hands. "Don't you dare make me cry. You know I'm hormonal."

"I do now."

I draw her closer and place a chaste kiss on her forehead.

She smells fresh and soapy—she must have already showered this morning. It suits her.

"But please go and get dressed for my sanity's sake."

She's chuckling all the way to the hall door when she turns and smiles back at me. Her gaze flicks down to my cock and back up again before she rolls her eyes and disappears into her bedroom.

These are going to be the longest months of my life.

TWELVE
ZOE

THREE MONTHS *later*

I'M SO BORED.

Work has all but dried up, and I spend my days surfing the Internet and looking for something to spark a new idea.

At the same time, morning sickness has lingered, although it doesn't bother me every day.

And I have a bump.

It popped out about a month ago, and has only grown.

Next week we have a scan to make sure everything's in the right place. Hearing the heartbeat made the pregnancy real—seeing the baby together will be on a whole other level.

I've also taken to stalking Declan.

Hormones swirling in my system have made me lust after him something chronic, although seeing him every morning in that low-slung pair of pyjama pants hasn't helped. It's like the man is almost allergic to clothing when he gets out of bed.

My vibrator has never been busier.

And I've never been so glad that this apartment has sturdy walls that keep the sound in.

For his part, he's been just as charming and courteous as he was when he first moved in. He begrudgingly lets me cook when I really want to, but most nights he's the chef and he won't ever let me wash the dishes. I'm kind of impressed he's lasted this long, but he's showing no signs of being unhappy.

In fact he seems to enjoy being here more and more as my body changes and I'm now visibly pregnant.

I open my Declan stalking tab. He's in the shower and distracted, and I usually google him once a day to see what the news is saying about him.

No news is good news—there's not been any Declan updates in months, with the last one being his kiss with a 'mystery brunette' outside the Bellagio (spoiler alert—it was me!).

We might not be so lucky next time. Not that there are any plans for a repeat kiss.

I sigh and click through the pages. Usually I stop at the first couple because Declan shows up and interrupts me, but this time I keep going until something catches my eye, and I freeze.

Declan has a sex tape.

I thought I knew everything about him, but how did I miss something like that?

It takes some digging through fake links to find the real

thing—no wonder I haven't seen it. I didn't go much further than a basic search.

My eyes widen as I find the right link and click on it, Declan coming into focus right at the start. It's clear he doesn't know he's being filmed as he strips—not once even glancing in the direction of the camera.

I shouldn't be doing this. If he was filmed in secret, the person doing the filming didn't have consent, but I can't take my eyes off him.

My memories of our night together aren't the clearest.

We'd both been drinking, and I remember the sex being really, really good, but not much of the detail.

His cock is huge.

That? That was inside me?

The woman he's with smiles, and next thing she's sucking on it like there's no tomorrow. It's almost hypnotic. Up and down she goes.

You can't see Declan's face at this point, but he's definitely making sex noises.

I'm not paying any attention when my phone rings beside me. And I'm paying even less when Caitlin starts talking, I'm so mesmerised by what's on the screen.

"What are you doing?" she asks.

A loud groan comes from the laptop. I frantically press buttons on the keyboard.

"Are you watching porn?" She laughs. "I know it's been a while with being pregnant and all, but ..."

"Declan has a sex tape on the Internet," I whisper.

"He *what?*" She screeches. "And you're watching it?"

"I have to. It's the law or something."

"Oh my god." In the background I hear her tapping away.

"Wait. Are you looking it up? I don't know how I feel about this."

Caitlin chuckles. "There's no way I'm missing it."

I wriggle in my seat. This video's been viewed millions of times, but I'm not sure I'm comfortable with my best friend watching it. If I didn't know Declan, sure, but he's living in my home and everything's pointing to him being in my life for a long time to come.

"What *are* you doing?"

I jump and slam the laptop shut before fumbling with my phone and disconnecting Caitlin. "Just messing around on the Internet."

Declan twists my chair around until I'm facing him. "Uh-huh. Looking at my dick."

"I ... I ..." My cheeks burn.

His smirk just makes me mad. "It's okay, babe. I've got no issue with you checking out your property."

My eyes widen and he chuckles.

"As hot as that video is, I prefer the memory of *your* lips wrapped around it."

I lick my lips, desperate to get rid of that dry-mouth feeling that's just appeared.

"Jesus, Zoe. You have no idea how hot you are."

"I've got a confession to make," I whisper.

His eyebrows rise, and I swallow hard before continuing. "I ... I can't remember everything about that night."

Declan frowns. "You weren't that drunk."

"I think I was more drunk than I'd thought. I remember helping Caitlin back to her room, and I remember going to yours, but ..." I chew my bottom lip. "It's the rest that's a bit blurry. I mean, I haven't forgotten everything, but there are gaps."

His chests rises and falls like he's been running. "Maybe I'll just have to remind you."

I swear to God my core pulses. My brain might be fuzzy, but my body definitely remembers him.

What I need to do is change the subject.

"Where did that tape come from?" I ask.

He blows out a long breath. "Do you really want to know about my murky past?"

I gaze into his blue eyes. "It's important. For the sake of the baby."

Declan snorts. "Really?"

"No. I'm just nosey." I laugh, and he grins, shaking his head.

"My first marriage breakup came as a huge surprise. She'd become convinced I was cheating on her."

"And you weren't?"

He shakes his head. "I was young and new to Hollywood. She didn't like being photographed in public, so she stayed home while I went to every event I could. Networking is such a big part of this scene. We met in Los Angeles. She knew who I was and what I wanted from my career when I started, but the bigger the role, the more she withdrew."

"Is it her in the video?"

He taps me on the nose. "Patience, grasshopper. I told you that I'd tell you everything about my life. No, it's not her."

I bite my bottom lip. I'm impatient—I know, but being so close to him when he smells so good is driving me crazy. I've read that pregnancy can make you horny, but when the father of your baby who's been so attentive is right next to you? I'd jump his bones in a heartbeat.

Not that I can tell him that.

"Anyway, things didn't last. We were both young and stubborn. I didn't want to miss any chance of furthering my career. She hated the lifestyle. When she left me, that was my first real walk on the wild side. I partied, I had a lot of sex, and I got so caught up in it that when a woman I'd fucked and ghosted released a video of us, I barely even cared."

I gape. I'm not stupid—I knew he had a reputation, but this? I'm not sure what to make of it.

"That was the first time I went to rehab. I got my shit together for a while, and I got a restraining order to stop her from sharing it, but by then it was all over the Internet."

"That's revenge porn."

He nods. "It is. Back then, there weren't really any laws against it like that. I did all I could to stop it. But it's been a long time since it was released, and I ended up doing far more damage to my career than that video ever did."

The mood has definitely cooled in this room. It's clear Declan's a man with many regrets. I just hope our baby and I don't get added to that list.

"You know, Zoe, if you ever want a re-run of that night—I'm right here." His deep voice rumbles and it's like a signal to my very hungry vagina.

I want him. Oh God, how I want him. Is it a good idea? Probably not, but I don't care anymore.

Declan O'Leary is my baby daddy, and I want him inside me again.

THIRTEEN
ZOE

HE'S NOT FINISHED.

"It doesn't have to be more if you don't want it to be. It could just be sex." He says it so matter-of-factly, I could almost believe him. But I'm not sure it could just be sex with Declan. Not now. "If you lie down on your bed, I'll eat your pussy. I fucking loved doing that."

My eyebrows rise, and the ache in my core grows. One of the things I remember very clearly was the morning after when Declan went down on me. I've never met a man as enthusiastic when giving oral sex.

"Declan," I whimper.

"Is that a yes?" He smiles that panty-dropping smile, and I know I'm done for. How can I say no?

My hormones are raging—I've never craved sex the way I do right now. And I'm sure a lot of it is to do with the fact that Declan's right here. He cooks. He cleans. He's hot as sin.

And I'm down for a refresher course in that man's body.

He chuckles as I all but sprint for the bedroom—which is no mean feat when your centre of gravity is changing.

I pull back the covers and flop on the bed, and Declan follows, shaking his head.

"How long have you been feeling this way?" he asks.

"Forever. Now get over here and do this."

"Do what?" He smirks.

I wave my hands in the general direction of my body. "All of this."

He chuckles. "Get naked and I'll do whatever you want me to."

I've never stripped so fast. Despite my anxiety about my pregnant body, I want his hands on me—his tongue on me—his ...

Declan's out of his clothes faster than I am, and he climbs into bed beside me.

He runs his hand down the curve of my belly.

"I still can't quite believe you're growing my baby in there." His tone is so soft, caring, it's enough to bring tears to my eyes. *Stupid hormones.*

"I'm glad you're my baby daddy," I whisper.

He laughs softly. "There will probably come a time when you take that back."

I shake my head. "No. I have faith in you."

Declan nuzzles my neck. "Saying things like that just make you even hotter."

I roll my eyes. "I'm like a beached whale right now, and there are still four months to go."

"Stop that right now. You're gorgeous. Pregnancy suits you."

"Do you really think so?"

His warm gaze makes my heart beat faster. "Of all the women I've ever met in my life, I'm glad it's you having my baby. You're beautiful, smart, and rocking that baby bump."

I snort. "Stop it."

"It's true." He places his hand over my belly button. "I can't stop looking at you, even when you're wearing clothes. The morning sickness has been a bit rough, but you're glowing, and I hope that's because I'm making sure you're getting enough rest."

I tilt my head. "I'm sure there are some activities I could do more of."

His lips quirk into a smile. "Like what?"

"Can I be honest?"

Desire flares in his eyes. "I'd like that."

"I keep thinking about sex with you and how good it was. Maybe the finer details aren't there, but I know that night was amazing. And you told me off for walking around in my underwear, but those pyjama pants you wear are ..." I hold up my fingers to my mouth and smack my lips together. "Chef's kiss."

He chuckles. "I'll keep wearing them if you like them."

"So much for keeping this platonic. I'm not complaining though." I laugh.

Declan shrugs, his hand drifting down toward my pussy. "I'm not sure that was ever really going to work. Not when there's this crazy attraction between us."

"I didn't ... I didn't know if you felt the same way." Tears prick my eyes.

He meets my gaze. "I've been trying to resist you since the day I moved in."

"Is this really a good idea?"

"Are you really talking yourself out of sex?"

I swallow hard. He's right. He's what fantasies are made of and he's offering me no-strings sex. Oh, who am I kidding? There are strings—big strings—but can we look past those just so he can pleasure me when I want it?

My head is telling me no, but my vagina has other ideas.

"Sorry, I'm just ... I'm all over the place right now. You know, hormones," I shrug.

"You mean you're horny?" He smirks.

"Yes." I pout. "And you and those pyjama pants ..." I let out an exaggerated sigh.

"I'll wear them all day, every day if it makes you happy."

My eyebrows rise. "You would?"

"That's what I'm here for." His fingers brush against my clit, and I almost explode on the spot. "There's also another thing I'm here for right now."

"Yes please." I'm not above begging.

"You only have to ask. Not this time. I know what you want, but if you'd like a repeat ..."

"I'll remember that."

He slides a finger into me. "So ready." He slides another finger into me and my lips part. "So needy."

As he runs his fingers back over my clit, I grasp his bicep. His eyes never leave mine as he rubs the swollen nub and I fight the urge to close my eyes.

It all happens so fast that it catches me by surprise. And then I'm falling. He slides his arm underneath my shoulders and holds me close as waves of pleasure hit my body.

When I finally feel like I can breathe out, he's between my legs in an instant.

All I can do is stare at his gaze eating me up before he leans down and takes long licks then settles his tongue on my clit.

He sucks gently on it and I shudder.

I'm still so sensitive from his touch, but he makes light work of my second orgasm, licking, sucking, lapping at my pussy.

"Just as sweet as you were the first time around," he says.

"I thought pregnancy might change things."

He emerges from between my thighs. "If anything, you taste even better."

My cheeks burn red, and his lips twist into a smile.

"I love going down on you, Zoe. Can't get enough of it." He moves up the bed until he's beside me and rolls me onto my side. His hand goes back to my clit, rubbing it while I arch my back against him.

"I need you inside me."

"Do I need a condom?"

"I..."

He places a kiss behind my ear. "I get tested regularly for insurance purposes. I'm clear."

"Then, no. You can't get me pregnant again."

His hot breath wafts across the back of my neck as he laughs. "You have a point."

Lifting my leg, he eases himself into me. I let out a contented sigh.

"Are you okay?" He asks gently.

"Yes. I'm full of you."

He chuckles again, moving slowly back and forth. "Any time you need me, you can have me."

The sex that first night was frantic.

Tonight, not so much.

"You feel good," he murmurs. "Perfect."

"Touch me."

He runs his hand up to my breast, his fingers brushing my nipple, and I groan.

"Sensitive?"

"Very."

"I'll remember that." With a gentle squeeze, he drops his hand to my belly, his light touch warming my heart. "I love touching you."

He runs his hand up my body again, his lips pressed against my neck, his hot breath on my skin. I close my eyes and *feel*.

Declan moves in and out of me, fulfilling my need for him. I don't want anyone else.

Is this a turning point in our relationship?

After how we've grown emotionally closer these last few months—how we depend on each other, I'm not sure this could ever *just* be sex for me.

Could Declan feel the same?

He brushes his fingers over my body until they're down to my clit. My body's so responsive to his touch, and I arch my back against him.

"That's it, baby. Let me give you what you need."

It's all too much—his cock inside me, his fingers rubbing, and I'm in sensory overload.

"Come with me, Zoe. I know you want to." His hot breath on my neck sends shivers down my spine.

My core pulses as my world explodes.

"That's it. I can't hold on anymore." Declan groans behind me, thrusting hard before slowing.

We lie together, his softening cock still inside me.

It takes a moment to catch my breath, and Declan kisses my bare shoulder.

"Are you okay?" he asks.

"Wonderful."

He rolls me back so I'm facing him. His gaze sweeps my face, the affection in his eyes warming my heart.

Kissing me softly, he then gets out of bed and goes to the bathroom, returning with a warm washcloth to clean me. Then I'm asleep within minutes.

I barely register the rest of the night.

His warm lips brush against my bare shoulder. "Good morning."

"That was the best sleep I've had in ages." I let out a yawn.

"Me too. It's not been easy sleeping right across the hall from you."

I roll over so I'm facing him. "Does this mean you'll be sleeping here every night?" I bite my bottom lip.

"Only if you want me to. I won't say no if you that's what you need."

"I'd like that."

He reaches up and pushes my hair behind my ear. "Then, your wish is my command."

"Why are you so perfect?"

Declan chuckles. "I'm not. You are."

Swoon.

FOURTEEN
DECLAN

I'VE BEEN in Zoe's bed every night for the past two weeks.

But we're not together—not in any kind of official sense. I'm not sure how I feel about that, but we're satisfying each other's needs and it's bringing us closer. And not just in a physical sense.

I frown when Nikki's name comes up on my phone. She hasn't called in a while, and I thought I'd finally gotten through to her that I'm done.

But maybe she's calling just to say hi—after all we have been pretty close.

For the first time in a long time, I answer the call.

"Nikki?"

"Don't hang up. I'm not trying to get you onto any other project. It's about your last one."

I roll my eyes. The name of that movie has changed several times and I've lost track. I'm not sure I really care anymore.

"What about it?"

"Have you seen the news about Jessie Lane?"

I freeze. Jessie was my co-star on that movie—her career's been on the same trajectory as mine for other reasons. I'd heard she was difficult to work with, but she was really lovely. Although she was having trouble with a stalker at the time too.

"Nope. I've been busy with other things. What's up?"

"She was stabbed by her stalker. She's okay, and they caught the woman who did it, but the production company want to capitalise on the publicity and have a small premiere for the movie in a couple of weeks. And then they've sold it to Netflix for streaming."

I choke out a laugh. "You're kidding. Is she really okay?"

"Apparently so. I don't have much detail on it."

"Wow. Poor thing."

"Yeah. Her stalker tracked her all the way to New Zealand and stabbed her there. I'd love to know more, but the detail just isn't available. But anyway, what do you say?"

"About?"

"Attending the premiere. Small red carpet. Limited screening. And it's in your contract, so you're obligated."

I huff out a breath. "I'll think about it."

"I'll send you the details."

An hour later, my phone rings again. *Jessie Lane.*

I gave her my number while we were working together just in case she needed support while dealing with her stalker.

"Jessie," I say as I answer the call.

"Declan. How are you?"

"I should ask you the same. I've not seen the news, but my agent tells me you've been through an ordeal."

She sighs. "I'm okay. But that stalker I had hurt me. It's in the past now, and I just wanted to talk to you and see if you were going to this premiere."

I grimace. "I probably should."

Jessie pauses. "Do you have a date?"

Wait.

Is she asking me out?

Zoe and I haven't discussed any of this. Can we go on dates while she's pregnant with my baby? How would I feel if she went out with another man?

The idea of it doesn't sit comfortably with me.

"I ... uhhh."

She laughs. "Relax, Declan. I'm not asking you out. I just ..." Her tone changes, and the bounce she usually has disappears. "I just need a friend."

Shit.

"Any other time, and I'd say yes. But ..."

"Oh. You have a girlfriend?"

I frown. "Well, no, but ..." I blow out a long breath. "It's complicated. There's a woman I met in Las Vegas. You remember that trip I had planned when we finished the film? I had a one-night stand which has turned into, well, I'm not sure what it is yet."

She's switched off from what I'm saying judging by the uh-huhs and the hmms that come from her after that, but I spill everything before we finish the call.

I'm sure she didn't listen, but telling someone helped a lot.

ZOE'S NOSE is buried in a book when I walk into the living room. The afternoon sun floods in the window behind her, bathing her in light. She's so effortlessly beautiful.

"Zoe?"

Looking up, she blinks as if shaking herself out of her thoughts.

"I've got a movie premiere coming up, and I wondered if you wanted to go with me."

"You do?" She puts down her book and stretches. "What movie is that for? I thought you said the last one went straight to DVD."

I shrug and walk toward her, then drop onto the other end of the couch. "Apparently not. My co-star was stalked and attacked—the studio want to cash in on the publicity."

She grimaces. "That seems a bit gruesome."

"It won't be a blockbuster, but it's a free night out with a red carpet."

Zoe taps her forefinger on her chin. "It gives me an excuse to buy a new gown. I mean, it's fancy, right?"

I grin. "I'll be wearing a tux."

"Swoon." She laughs and all the tension rolls out of me. "It's a shame I can't drink. They'll have champagne and things, won't they?"

"They will, but seeing as you can't drink, I won't either."

I'm not sure she'll realise how big a sacrifice I'm making. It's been years since I've coped with one of these nights without the calming influence of a drink.

"You don't have—" She starts.

"I do."

Her lips turn down into a frown. "Okay."

"I'm not doing anything that risks whatever this is with us."

Zoe's eyes widen.

I shift closer to her. "I think you know as well as I do that there's something more here than sex. I'm not going to do anything put that in danger."

She licks her lips. "I ... I think the same."

"I'm relieved." I smile. "Although the sex is pretty damn good."

I could eat out on her laughter for years.

FIFTEEN
DECLAN

PREGNANCY IS A ROLLER COASTER. And I say that even though I'm not the one who's pregnant.

As time goes on, Zoe gets more emotional.

Her hormones seem so up and down, and I'm just along for the ride.

We've got our trip to LA planned, and I'm hoping that will put a smile on her face. The morning sickness mostly went away but still rears its ugly head from time to time, yet she tries to brave it out.

It makes me want to be with her even more.

I do whatever I can to make her life easier.

I'm standing in the bathroom, running her a bath, when footsteps fall behind me.

I turn. She's behind me in a big pale blue fluffy robe, and I shoot her a smirk. "Come and get in this bath, babe. The water's fine."

Her weepy eyes are full of some unidentifiable emotion.

"Thank you."

Zoe's a weepy, emotional mess and I've never felt so protective of anyone in my life. Her belly's swollen with my baby, and more than ever, I want more with her.

She's mine.

She flicks her gaze between me and the tub.

"Want me to join you?"

Her nose twitches and she nods before bursting into tears again.

"Oh, baby, you are really not having a good day, are you?" I wrap my arms around her and hold her while she cries on my shoulder.

"I'm just so tired," she whispers.

"I can't wait until they're here." I press a kiss to Zoe's temple. "Let me help you undress." I tug off my T-shirt and drop my jeans to the floor.

Her lips twitch. "When you were attending all those fancy movie premieres, I bet you never thought you'd one day be standing in a bathroom half-naked and pampering a pregnant crying woman."

Chuckling, I pull at her robe's belt. "A very beautiful pregnant woman who's having *my* baby." I roll her robe off her shoulders. She's wearing a tank top and panties underneath, and her curvy body's enough to make me salivate.

I drop my boxer shorts to the ground, and her gaze drops with them before flicking back up my body. "I'm all yours, Zoe. If you'll have me."

She sniffs. "It's hard to focus while you're standing there naked."

I grin. "It's my big dick, isn't it?"

Her nose wrinkles, and she dissolves into laughter. It does my heart good to hear her after all the tears. "That is one of the things I like about you."

I climb into the bathtub and hold out my hand. "Care to join me?"

Zoe blushes, unclasping her bra and letting it fall to the floor. After slipping out of her panties, she reaches for my hand and steps into the tub.

"We need to go to LA for this premiere, and so I can show you my house. My tub's a lot bigger than this one."

Her eyes flash with amusement. "Why would we need a bigger tub?"

"Because there's no room to fuck in here."

Her eyebrows rise, but she says nothing.

I sit in the bathtub and she turns around and rests between my legs, leaning back against my torso.

"I'm sorry I'm such a mess," she says, leaning her head back on my shoulder.

I kiss her temple. "You're not. Your body is adapting to this massive change."

"It'll keep changing until you don't want me anymore."

I run the loofah over her belly. "I love your body no matter what. You have no idea what it means to me to see you like this. You're beautiful."

"And then giving birth will be messy and—"

"And another beautiful thing where we get our baby in the end, and you and I can work out what we're doing next."

She laughs softly. "You're not going to let me be negative at all, are you?"

"There's nothing to be negative about. I'm not sure I've ever been so content. You're what's been missing in my life."

Zoe raises her hand and lays it on mine. "How do you always know the right things to say?"

"Because this is meant to be. This pregnancy. Us. I'm not sure I ever believed in fate, but I do now because we were supposed to meet, you and I."

She hums her agreement. "I like the way you think."

We sit in the quiet of the bathroom as I gently wash her. Her head flops against my shoulder.

"I think it must be time to get out," I murmur.

"No," she moans.

"You're falling asleep. I'm going to tuck you into bed."

"Only if you join me."

"You know I will."

By the time we get out of the tub, dry off, and get dressed, she's yawning. A good night's sleep is what she needs.

I guide her to the bed, and she sits on the end.

"I love you," I say.

Her breath hitches, and her eyes fill with tears. The way things have been lately, I'm not sure if it's due to hormones or my declaration or a combination of both.

"I'm not perfect. I've got two failed marriages behind me and a sex tape floating around the Internet. I'm an alcoholic. I'm the last man you could ever really want to be your baby daddy." I take a breath. "But I'm yours, Zoe. I think I was from the moment we met, and I just didn't know it."

This is the least romantic way to tell her, but I can't pretend my past doesn't exist. It's not pretty.

"I don't need you to be perfect," she whispers. "But I need you to keep yourself together for us."

I nod. "I will. The last time I had a drink was the night we were first together, and I'll get help. The rest I can't change, but I can be a better man going forward. I just want you and our baby. We can live anywhere you want, and I'll do whatever it takes. I love you."

She blinks rapidly, but tears roll down her cheeks. "I love you too. You haven't missed a step since you've been here."

I gather her into my arms and kiss her tears away. "All I need is you two. I never knew what I was missing out on until now. I don't need Hollywood. I don't need the career pressure."

"Are you sure? I want to keep working for myself after the baby's born. I love it. But I did worry about how I'd balance everything." She sniffs.

"Whatever you want, babe. I'll stay home and change diapers and be a dad." I suck in a breath. "Holy shit. I'm going to be a dad."

Zoe laughs, and it's music to my ears. "Yes, yes you are." She wraps her arms around my waist and rests her head on my shoulder.

"You two are my reason for going on. You know that, right? You make being sober easy." I plant a kiss on the top of her head. "You came along right when I needed you."

"Don't say that."

"Meant to be, remember?"

She smiles. "Maybe you're right."

"I know I am."

SIXTEEN
DECLAN

MY SKIN THRUMS WITH EXCITEMENT.

This is it. This is me.

Today's the day I introduce Zoe to my life.

We taxi from the airport up into the Hollywood Hills where my refuge from the world is. She has no idea just how big the estate is or how much I want to share it with her.

When we pull up to the wrought-iron gate, she gasps. "This is your house?"

I grin. It's big and ostentatious—especially when it's just me living here. But I love it. I'd be devastated if I ever had to give it up.

This was the hideaway I bought with my biggest movie cheque. An Edwardian mansion in the Hollywood Hills wasn't where I'd pictured myself living, but the moment I saw it, I knew I had to have it.

It's huge, it's quirky, and it's all mine.

The gates open, and we drive up to the entrance where I

help her out the car and then grab our luggage. I unlock the front door, and push it open.

"This is insane." Zoe's eyes are wide as she looks around the entranceway. I can't help but smile. She could afford a place like this, but she's so self-conscious about her wealth, she'd never do it.

Me, on the other hand? I've always liked the finer things in life. And a big house in the Hollywood Hills fits the picture.

I frown at the sound of heels clipping on the tiled floor and turn toward the staircase.

A glance back at Zoe makes my heart sink. Her gaze is fixed on the blonde making her way toward us.

Annabelle.

My second ex-wife.

Who definitely *shouldn't* be in this house..

"What in the ever-loving FUCK are you doing here?" I yell.

She recoils. "You weren't here. I thought—"

"You thought wrong. Get your shit and get out. And return the key you're not supposed to have."

Annabelle tilts her head, and a soft smile spreads on her lips. "Declan, baby."

"We've been divorced for *five* years. You got more than you were entitled to. Get the fuck out of my house."

"I need somewhere to stay."

"You have friends. Go crash with one of them. What happened to the house you got in the divorce?"

She pouts. "It's complicated."

"Just get out, Annabelle. We were done a long time ago."

Fixing her gaze on Zoe, she smirks. "Don't think you'll get a ring on his finger."

I glare at her. "Zoe's the best thing that's ever happened to me. The only thing I regret is the ring I put on *your* finger. Biggest. Mistake. Ever."

Her nostrils flare, and I know I've hit her hard.

While I have so many regrets about my first marriage—Ciara didn't deserve the way this life chewed her up and spat her out—Annabelle was a big old drunken mistake. I'm not sure I was sober at any point in our relationship. That's on me, but she was just as toxic, and we were bad together. There was never a future there. And when we divorced, she did her best to suck me dry, but our pre-nup held tight and she only got what she was entitled to. It was still more than enough to set her up for life. If she's run out of money, she's only got herself to blame.

"Get out of my house. Text me where you're staying so I can send you whatever you brought here. I'll be having the locks changed so you can't get back in."

Her eyes flare with anger and she storms toward the front door.

"Good riddance," I call.

The doorjamb rattles as she slams it shut, and I snort. "I'm so sorry, Zo."

I turn toward her.

Instead of the upset woman I expect to find, Zoe's got her lips clamped together as if she's trying not to laugh.

"I'm glad *you* find it funny."

Zoe snorts, and then holds her hand over her nose, her

mouth falling open in horror. It's enough to set me off, and I grasp her arm, laughing right along with her.

"So, that was your ex-wife?" she asks.

"One of them."

She rolls her eyes. "Oh, Lordy. What *have* I got myself into?"

"I haven't seen the other one in years. Annabelle is the only pain in my ass, though I'll make it clear she needs to stay far away from me. She's got a nerve coming here. She never even lived here when we were married."

Zoe's expression softens. "She didn't?"

"No. This is and has always been my place. We lived in an apartment together. I don't even know how she got a key, but I'll sure as hell be finding out." I huff out a breath. "Take a seat in the living room and I'll organise some coffee and something to eat."

Zoe draws closer, cupping my face between her hands. "It's not your fault. I'm okay."

The tension eases, and I roll my shoulders. She always knows how to disarm me. "I'm sorry, babe. She sets me on edge."

"I can see. But she's gone now." After a gentle kiss, she heads toward the living room, and I race up to my bedroom, taking two stairs at a time.

Relief floods through me that she doesn't appear to have slept in my bed. It wouldn't feel right bringing Zoe here if she had. I'd need to burn the mattress.

One of the guest bedrooms is trashed. The bedding is a mess. And food wrappers litter the room. It's like she'd hunkered down in here and barely left.

Maybe that's what happened here.

She must have been counting on me not coming here anytime soon. I guess it has been months since I was in town, and that's how my life has always been—here then gone for shoots and promo.

I'll talk to the housekeeper when she's in about cleaning up. She can have a bonus for dealing with this crap.

Thankfully the kitchen is stocked—so the housekeeper has been in while Annabelle's here. I'll have to address that too.

After making some coffee and a sandwich for Zoe, I head out the back to where my groundskeeper lives. He's the holder of spare keys, and I want answers.

He gives me a cautious smile as I approach.

"How did Annabelle get in?" There's no point in beating around the bush.

At least he has the decency to look sheepish. "I gave her a key. It's completely my fault."

I set my jaw. "What on earth did she tell you to convince you to do that?"

He looks at the floor.

"What did she promise you?"

Charlie's been a part of my life for years. Once I bought this place, I needed a groundskeeper who could maintain it—any effort on my part would have been a token gesture, and there's far too much garden for me to deal with it.

"She said you'd given her permission to stay—told me the man she was with had been stalking her and she needed somewhere safe."

I sigh. "You didn't call me."

"What can I say? I'm a soft touch."

I don't have the heart to let him go. And I get it. The only wife he ever knew me with was Annabelle, even though she never lived in this house. He's an older man she's taken advantage of.

"No one stays here unless I bring them."

He nods. "I'm sorry, Declan. Maybe I'm getting too old in the tooth for this. I only did it because I knew she used to be your wife."

"We've been divorced for five years. She's not my problem anymore." I grasp his shoulder. "Don't let one bad judgment put you off. You know how much I value the way you look after this estate."

He rises his gaze to meet mine. "How long are you staying this time?"

I grin. "Not long. I'm just here for a premiere. I'll bring my lady out to meet you at some point. We'll be staying for a few days."

"I'm happy for you."

"Thanks. I'm going to head back in, but please, Charlie. No one gets access to this house unless it's me or my lady."

He gives me a nod, and I walk back inside. Zoe looks up from her spot on the couch and smiles. "Everything okay?"

"It will be in a minute."

Her brows knit, but I sit beside her and pull her toward me, kissing her with every bit of passion I can muster. She laughs against my lips before I deepen the kiss.

When I let her up for air, I hold her close, and she laughs softly.

I run my hand over her head. "Now everything's right with the world."

SHE SIGHS CONTENTEDLY when she climbs into my big, comfortable bed.

"Your ex didn't sleep in here, did she?"

I shake my head. "No, she slept down the hall. The room's a mess. My housekeeper will sort it tomorrow."

She laughs. "Housekeeper. Groundskeeper. Assistant. It's like a foreign language."

"I've never gone too crazy. I like doing things for myself."

Zoe snuggles down under the covers. "Come here and show me."

After sliding into bed, I spoon my naked body behind hers, placing my hand on her swollen belly.

"Declan?" Zoe lets out a yawn.

"Yes, sweetheart?"

"Did you know when you do that, the baby settles. It's like you have the magic touch."

I chuckle, kissing her bare shoulder. "She knows her daddy already."

"She?"

"We're having a girl."

Zoe laughs softly. "So confident."

"A father knows."

"You're so full of it."

I nuzzle her behind her ear, and she sighs. "Maybe, but don't tell our daughter."

"Only three months until we find out for real. Our baby is modest. Unlike you."

Laughter bursts from me, and she grunts, rolling onto her back before I help her to get to her other side. "I asked for that," I smirk.

"You can't help yourself. I'm beginning to think you'd give up clothing if you could."

Her blue eyes twinkle with mischief. I'm so crazy about her. To think I could have missed all this if she hadn't fallen pregnant.

When I say nothing, her brow furrows.

"I really love you. You know that, right?" I say. Her eyes fill with tears, and I know I've said the wrong thing.

"What did you do?" she asks.

"Shit. Nothing. I just meant that I really love you. And I know things were weird at first, but I'm glad you're pregnant. I'm glad it brought us together, and I'm so stupidly happy—more than I've ever been."

A smile shifts her lips.

"I just hope I'm making you happy."

She nods. "These past months have been wonderful. I love you so much."

Her lips, just begging to be kissed, twitch. I smile before claiming them with my own, pouring my love into her. Being with Zoe has made me realise just how much I've been missing all my life—it's always been about the surface and not what's underneath.

What I have with Zoe is real.

The kiss deepens, and when I finally let her up for air, a wicked grin appears on her face.

"Uh-oh. What's that for?" I ask.

"Now you've woken me up, and you're already naked, so ..."

SEVENTEEN
ZOE

TONIGHT'S the night of Declan's premiere, and my stomach is a bundle of nerves.

I sit on the bed, and open my laptop to call Caitlin.

We've kept in touch with Zoom, but it's not the same. Declan's good company, but there are times when I really need my best friend.

She squeals when I show her how my bump is growing. I hate that she's not here and sharing this with me, but at least we can talk via video.

"So, how's life with the sexy Declan?" Caitlin tilts her head and smiles.

"Amazing." I sigh.

"I know you. You're waiting for that bubble to burst, right?"

I hesitate. She's right. I'm sure I'd be fooling myself if I thought whole thing I have going with Declan would last forever. His past reputation doesn't support the idea of him sticking around for long—although this is the first time a child's been involved. "I guess."

"Whatever happens, I'm here. You know that, right?"

I nod. "I know."

"So, what are you up to now?"

"Declan's got a movie premiere tonight. Nothing huge, but I'm going with him."

Her eyes widen. "Lucky bitch."

I laugh. "It's pretty crazy. I only just found out that he has an assistant. He doesn't do much because Declan does his own thing, but he organised a gown and for my makeup and hair to be done before we go tonight."

"Exciting!"

"It is. I'm feeling pretty good now—the morning sickness seems to have passed. Until now I've been crawling into bed early because I'm so tired. But I'm looking forward to tonight. What are you doing?"

She lets out a big sigh. "Brandon's at a training camp this weekend, but he's back on Monday. I hate it when he goes away. Apart from the other players' wives, I don't really know anyone here yet."

"It'll happen."

"I miss *you*."

"I miss you too."

"Zoe, are you ready for hair and makeup?" Declan calls from the living room.

"I've got to go and become a princess."

Caitlin laughs. "Have fun. Get loads of photos and send them to me."

"Will do." I blow her a kiss and close my laptop.

I'm not used to being fussed over. The only time I've ever had my makeup done was when I posed for a headshot for my company website.

By the time I get downstairs, I'm nervous, but Declan greets me with a smile and leads me into the living room.

They've taken over my work desk—which I told Declan was the best place to use for this, and set up a mirror against the wall so I can see what's happening.

"Zoe, this is Tatum and Maxine. They're here to do your hair and makeup."

I take a deep breath and sit down before they get to work. Declan takes up a position in a chair so he can watch proceedings.

And when it's all done, I look at myself in the mirror and smile.

"You look beautiful," Declan says. "Not that you don't all the time."

I laugh. "Thank you for this."

"I'm enjoying being able to pamper my girl. Go and get your gown on. I'll be there in a minute to zip you up."

After placing a kiss on his cheek, I head back up to the bedroom and sigh a little at my gown hanging on the back of the door. As I drop it over my head, the beautiful navy fabric flows over me. It's perfect. Everything's perfect.

The click of the door tells me Declan's arrived, and he plants a kiss on the nape of my neck as he zips me up.

"Give me five and I'll be ready," he says.

"I'll believe it when I see it." I laugh.

When he reappears minutes later, fiddling with his cufflinks, I catch my breath. Declan O'Leary in grey trackpants is a sight—Declan O'Leary in a tux is devastatingly gorgeous.

"I'm ready when you are," he says.

"Any time."

He finishes adjusting his sleeves and holds out an arm for me to take. "Let's go, beautiful."

By the time we get to the limo parked outside, I'm trembling, but he's there with his hand in mine, giving it a reassuring squeeze.

"Nervous?" he asks.

I nod.

"I'll be with you the whole way. There'll be a few minutes while I have some photos taken, but Nikki will be around, and she'll be with you if I can't."

I draw in a deep breath. I've not met Nikki yet, but Declan seems to think I'll like her. She's been a part of his life for a long time and he says she's practically family to him. Given his real family turned their backs on him, I'm glad he has her. Although her presence in his life sparks my interest. If I'm honest, I'm a little jealous. It's hard not to be when Declan's lived the life he has. But I'm it for him now—me and our baby.

I have to hold onto that.

When we arrive, Declan gets out first and then turns back, holding his hand out for me to take. Once I'm on the footpath, I smooth down my skirt, thankful that it's full and hides my baby belly as the photographers' flashes go off.

I know the media will find out some time that Declan has a child, but I'd like that day to be as late as possible.

My nerves aren't helped by the fact that despite the fancy hair and makeup, I'm still feeling bloated.

"We just have to get past this first part of the red carpet and then we'll be out of the spotlight," he murmurs.

I squeeze his hand. "Where you lead, I follow."

"I love you."

I loop my arm through his, and he shepherds me through the throng of photographers, pausing every so often to smile and wave.

"You're doing well," he murmurs. "I just have to stop to pose for a few photos and then we'll be inside."

I nod.

He leads me toward a tall, blonde woman. She's gorgeous—probably around the same age as him, and she gives me a tight smile as we approach.

"Nikki. This is Zoe. Zoe, Nikki." Declan gives my arm a squeeze. "I'm entrusting you to Nikki's care while I go and get these photos taken."

"Zoe, you look lovely." Her smile relaxes as we watch Declan walk back to the red carpet and pose.

"Thank you. So do you."

She lowers her voice. "That dress covers your pregnancy well. I'm assuming that's what you were aiming for?"

I nod. "I thought it best."

"I'm surprised Declan's decided to support you. I thought ..." When I turn toward her, her cheeks are flushed.

"I gave him an out, you know. Told him he didn't have to be involved at all. I didn't need him. He chose to be with me."

She gives me a tight nod. "I know. He told me. It just came at a time when I was trying to get his career back on track. He needs this, Zoe. He'll be lost without the movies and these nights out."

"He's been perfectly happy for the past few months. I'm sure he'll tell me if he wants something more." My jaw tics in annoyance. She's not being rude—I get that she cares about him in a different way than I do, but the implication that I'm holding him back isn't lost on me. "I'd never stop Declan if he wanted to keep acting. It's up to him."

Her eyes widen. "Oh, I didn't—"

"He's not obligated to cancel what he's doing for me. I don't even know what the future holds, but …"

"How are my girls doing?" Declan cups my hip and places a kiss on my temple.

"Good." I smile at him, but his brows rise and I just know we'll be discussing this later.

"Why don't we go in?" he says.

He holds my hand the whole way, and all through the movie, squeezing tight when the love scenes appear on the screen. I can't deny that it's weird watching him on screen kissing and being in bed with another woman, but I know it's not real—*we're* real.

And when it's over, he joins Jessie Lane and the director on stage for a few questions before rejoining me and escorting me out a back door.

"Are you tired, or do you want to go for a drink somewhere?" Declan asks.

I raise an eyebrow at him. "A drink?"

"Nothing alcoholic. We just got invited to a private function after this."

I nod. "I'm fine. What do you mean *we*? You mean you."

He kisses me on the nose. "No, we. It'll all make sense when we get there."

"Where is it? I could do with putting my feet up."

He chuckles. "A little down the street. We can walk if you're up to it, or we can take the car. It's just a couple of minutes from here."

"Lead on, then."

Holding my hand, he takes me down the road and around the corner to a quiet little bar. He talks to the doorman briefly, and then the door is opened and we walk in.

"I've got a surprise for you," he says.

He steers me across the room until I see someone I definitely recognise.

Jessie Lane clasps her hands together and beams a bright smile at me. "You must be Zoe. I've heard nothing about you, but I hope we can change that."

I laugh.

She loops her arm in mine. "I've got people for you to meet. Zoe, this is Josh Carter and his wife, Delaney."

I say nothing—just stand there and blink. Declan nudges me with his elbow. After living with Declan for all these months, I thought I'd be better at this. But Josh Carter is huge—he's one of the biggest movie stars on the planet.

"Hi, Zoe." He holds out his hand, and I slide mine into his to shake it.

"I hear you're one of us." His wife claps her hands together.

"It's so nice to meet you," I croak. "One of us?"

She grins. "I'm from New Zealand too." Turning, she

waves a hand in the air toward a group of people. "Pania, Lana, come and meet Zoe."

"Your wife seems …" Declan says to Josh, "exuberant."

Josh chuckles. "But she's very good at adopting new people and taking them under her wing. I promise Zoe's in good hands."

"I have no doubt that she is." His eyes twinkle with mischief. "Zo, I think we've found our people."

"Once I heard where you were from, I knew I had to introduce you," Jessie says. "I just came back from New Zealand recently." Pain shoots across her expression.

"Oh, I think I heard about that. That was where you were …"

"Stabbed." She nods. "But I'm recovering and that woman is behind bars." She seems to be trying to force a smile. "I've got to go and talk to a few more people, but I'll leave you in Delaney's capable hands."

She takes the arm of a man standing nearby and guides him away from us.

I don't miss Delaney's worried look before she shifts her gaze to me and smiles.

"I hear you're pregnant. Let's get you off your feet." Delaney leads me to a booth, and I sink into the large comfortable seat.

"Ohhh, that's better."

She sits beside me. "Oh, I remember those days. At least you can sit down when you're watching the movie at a premiere."

Pania and Lana slide into the other side of the booth.

"Jessie not joining us?" I ask.

Delaney exchanges a look with Pania that I can't read.

"I hope she will, but our friendship is very new and pretty fragile. I think she feels more comfortable with Josh and Pania's other half, Reece."

"Oh."

Delaney spots a waitress and waves to get her attention. "Let's get some drinks and chat. It's so nice to meet you."

"It's nice to meet you too. I have to admit this is all a little overwhelming."

Her smile is so genuine and kind, I really do feel like I've landed on my feet here. "I get it. It took me some time to adjust to this life. But I think once you make friends, it's a lot easier."

After we order drinks, she leans back in her seat. "Let's get some gossip in before the boys finish talking shop."

"Is that what they're doing?"

She shrugs. "I assume so. That's the only reason Josh comes to these things. He'd much rather be at home with me and the kids."

The drinks arrive, and I take a long sip of lemonade.

"So, spill the beans. How did you two get together?" Delaney takes a sip of her drink.

"Well …" My cheeks burn, but these are good people. I'm at ease with them already which has to be a good sign—apart from Caitlin, it's been tough to click with people here. "We met in Vegas."

Her eyes widen. "Ooh, we want to do a girls' weekend there, but haven't got to it yet."

"Do it. Just don't get too drunk like my bestie did. We were supposed to be having fun over two nights, but she went overboard the first night and was out for the count for most of the time. Declan rescued us."

"Rescued you?" Pania asks.

I nod. "After he helped get her back to the hotel room, we ... uhh .... got to know each other."

"Oh." She leans back in her chair. "Good for you, girl. He's gorgeous."

"So are your men. I feel like I fell into a man-candy store."

Lana laughs. "Wait until Delaney plays them against each other and they start taking off their shirts to show off."

I shift my gaze to her. "Does that happen often?"

"Not really, but it's a sight to behold when it does." Delaney shoots me a wink and I laugh. "Where are you living? LA?"

I shake my head. "San Francisco. But I'm not sure if we'll stay there. I'm working out my contract after selling my company, and being pregnant I'm not doing much in the office. Declan and I really need to talk about it. He's got a huge house here. I wouldn't complain if we moved."

She grins. "You should do it. We help each other where we can. I've got children, and so has Lana, and we babysit for each other all the time. None of us really have family here, so we made our own village."

"That sounds wonderful," I say. "My parents are back in New Zealand, and I do have a bestie, but she's recently moved to Chicago, so I don't know if I'll see her that often."

Pania frowns. "I'm so sorry. Why did she move?"

"Her husband's in the NFL. He transferred teams, so she followed."

"That sucks. I mean, good on them, but it's hard when

your best friend moves away." Pania shifts her gaze to Delaney.

Delaney snorts. "Look at us. You followed me to LA."

Pania rolls her eyes. "I followed Reece to LA. You were just the icing on the cake."

I can't help but smile at their banter. Lana catches my eye and grins at me.

Music starts up, and I sigh a little at the sight of Josh Carter and Reece Evans walking toward us. Right behind them is Alex Stone, and I sigh a little more as Declan comes into focus. That tux is something else on him, but I can't wait to get him out of it.

One by one, the women leave the table to dance with their partners.

"Do you want to dance?" Declan asks.

"Would you be upset if I said no? I'm really comfortable here."

He grins. "No. I'll join you."

Sitting beside me, he leans over and places a kiss on my temple.

"So, what do you think?" Declan asks.

"About what?"

He waves his hand around. "This. Them. I feel comfortable here, but if you don't want—"

"I love it. They've all made me feel at home. I think this is what I've needed all along—friends."

He chuckles. "Don't let Caitlin hear you say that."

I shrug. "She knows she's my best friend. But she's also newly married and has her own life. There's no reason why she can't visit us here and meet everyone."

Declan nods slowly before a smile spreads across his lips. "Visit us here? Does that mean we're staying?"

"What can I say? I'm crazy in love with your house, and I can work from anywhere at this stage."

He slips his arms around my waist and pulls me as close as possible. "I'm crazy in love with you."

"And I'm about a hundred months' pregnant, so make the most of it while I'm feeling emotional."

Declan roars with laughter before kissing me tenderly. "I can't wait to hold our baby," he murmurs.

"You and me both."

EIGHTEEN

ZOE

I WANTED to be the one to tell Declan about the baby; I didn't want him to find out about it from the media—as unlikely as that was.

The day starts as normal with Declan and I tripping over each other while making breakfast—he insists he'll make it for me, I insist I'll make it myself.

And then his phone starts ringing off the hook.

"Is everything okay?" I ask as he rejects what's probably the twentieth call.

"Nikki's trying to get hold of me again. She's probably booked me a second-hand-car salesman gig."

I laugh. "Things can't be that bad." His dark look makes me stop laughing. "Really? It's that bad? I'm so sorry."

He sighs and drops onto the couch beside me. "It's fine. She's just struggling to get the hint even though I've told her point-blank I'm not interested in acting anymore."

"Not interested in acting or just not interested in all the bullshit that goes with it?"

He narrows his gaze. "What do you know of the bullshit?"

I shrug. "I'm not immune to reading gossip. I just thought—"

Anger flashes across his features before it cools, and his brows knit. "I messed up my own career. I took every opportunity that came my way and then self-destructed. There are things I'm so deeply ashamed of that I can never take back, and I'm done with doing terrible movies that aren't going anywhere but the discount bin."

Reaching out, I place my hand on his arm. "I had no idea."

"You and this baby—you're my fresh start. I don't want to talk to Nikki because she'll try to persuade me to make more shitty movies, and I don't want that."

His confession takes my breath away, and I gape at him. I had no idea his life was that bad—I'd looked him up on IMDB and apart from the big movies I recognised, it just looked like he'd always been busy. I never once thought that the movies he'd been in lately were bad or anything other than ... movies. He's mentioned his career sinking before, but I took that as hyperbole.

"Maybe you need to talk to her again and set her straight," I say.

"I've already done that."

"Want me to talk to her?"

His lips twitch into a smile. "You'd do that?"

I screw up my nose. "I kind of already did. She seemed to

imply I was what's holding you back. But you're my baby daddy, and you're already far more involved in my life than I'd ever thought you would be. Maybe I can insert myself in yours."

He chuckles. "I have zero issue with you inserting yourself in my life. And I'll definitely be talking to Nikki about what you just said."

As he leans forward, our gazes are locked together. My heart thrums when he closes in until his face is inches from mine.

He's such a good kisser.

I roll my eyes when his shrill ringtone breaks the moment.

"God damn it," Declan says. "Maybe I should get this."

"If she gives you a hard time, give the phone to me."

He smirks. "I don't know if I'd inflict your wrath onto Nikki."

When he answers, I can hear her voice through the phone. She's ranting, and his eyes grow wide.

"What? When?" Declan closes his eyes. This isn't a job offer. Something's gone wrong. But what? He's been so good with me. It's not like he's been out to bars or anything—he's been watching TV with me on the couch at night.

"I'll talk to Zoe. No. You don't need to." He sighs. "I know you care about how this affects her, but it's my job to make sure she's okay."

My Spidey senses start tingling.

When he hangs up the call, he just sits there for a moment in silence, anger rolling off him in waves.

What the hell has happened?

"The other day when we went grocery shopping. Someone took photos."

My eyebrows creep up.

"I should have thought about it. I've been off the radar for so long that I never thought the media would be interested in pictures of me."

I swallow hard.

"But apparently they're really interested in pictures of me with you. It's been a while since my last scandal ..."

A clap of laughter escapes me. "Scandal? We're two grown adults having a baby."

He nods. "Yes, but there are assumptions about our relationship."

I shrug. "Who cares?"

"I do. There are zoomed in photos of your baby bump which have gone viral. My much younger girlfriend having my baby is apparently news."

I clamp my lips together. "Much younger?"

He smirks. "There's already fifteen years between us, but you look younger than thirty, according to the stories. I'm a big, bad, cradle snatcher."

"Do the stories say that, or is that your wording?" I cock my head.

His eyes sparkle with amusement and he reaches for my hand. "That was my wording. To be honest, I barely notice the age gap. And I don't know how you do it, but you completely disarm me. I was so angry, but now ..."

"Shit happens. Just how bad is it?"

He drops his gaze. "Lots of speculation. Not all good. But

Nikki's calling my publicist, and they're going to conference call me so we can put out a statement."

Before he can stop me, I stand and make my way to my desk, opening up my laptop.

"What are you doing?" he asks.

"Seeing how bad it is."

It only takes a moment to find it posted by news agencies on Facebook, but scanning the comments makes me laugh.

"A lot of people seem to think I'm some kind of gold digger."

He snorts. "That's because they don't know you. It's funny considering I'm the one living in your apartment."

"I think it's the default thing people say about any woman."

Declan swivels my chair so I'm facing him. "You're amazing. Do you know that? A lot of other women would be angry about this."

"Want to know the truth?"

His dark gaze drills through me, and he nods.

"Remember when I told you I was pregnant, and I said I didn't want the media to be the ones to tell you? I'd anticipated this happening. It was just a matter of time—especially once you moved in with me."

His Adam's apple bobs as he gazes at me. It's all kinds of distracting. "I'm sorry they're calling you names."

"You should have seen some of the comments when I sold my company. It seems like no matter what the story is, people get personal."

He cups my cheek. "I can't imagine anyone with anything bad to say about you."

"They don't know me. And I'm okay with that. You and I know the truth. That's what matters."

"Do you know how amazing you are?" he asks.

I shrug. "You can tell me as often as you want."

He chuckles. "You are amazing, Zoe. You make me feel more like myself than I have in years. That night in Vegas, I never thought I'd find the woman I wanted to spend the rest of my life with."

I lean over and peck his cheek. "That's very sweet."

"You and this baby—you've turned everything upside down, and it's so *good*."

"So let's not let these photos get us upset. We'll get on with our lives, and ..." My phone rings—I know it's Caitlin. She has her own ringtone. I hold up a finger. "Hold that thought."

"Caitlin," I say as I answer the call.

"Oh my god, Zoe. I just saw the photos of you with Declan in the grocery store. Are you okay? I'm so angry."

"I'm fine."

She pauses. "Are you actually fine? Or are you fine, fine?"

"I'm actually fine." I laugh. "I think you're more angry than I am."

"That bitch reporter. I'm going to give her a piece of my mind."

"I love you, but it's okay. Declan's manager and publicist are going to work out a statement. I'll let them take care of it."

It's so Caitlin to defend me. I couldn't ask for a better best friend. I can just imagine her stamping around their apartment, flicking her blonde hair over her shoulder, ready to storm in and give attitude to everyone involved in this.

She growls, and I bite down a smile. "It makes me miss you more. If I was still there—"

"You'd be apart from Brandon and miserable. You're where you need to be, and so am I."

"Why are you so sensible?" She laughs.

"That's me."

"Hi, Caitlin," Declan calls in the background.

"Tell him if he lets the media say nasty things about you, I'll cut his balls off."

I burst out laughing. "He's doing his best to fix this. Promise."

"He'd better. I love you."

"Love you too."

"I'll leave you to it then. I just wanted to check in," she says.

I lean back on the couch and close my eyes. "Thank you. I really appreciate it. You need to come and visit me soon. We'll go to LA and I'll introduce you to some new people."

"New people?"

"I met Josh Carter," I whisper.

"Oh my god," she screeches, and I hold the phone away from my ear as Declan laughs.

"And Reece Evans."

"I'll tell Brandon he has to transfer to LA."

I laugh. "Just come and visit me soon."

"I will. Promise."

"Talk to you later?"

When she's gone, I put the phone down and lean my head on Declan's shoulder.

"She's got your back."
"Always."
"So do I."

NINETEEN
ZOE

Six weeks later

I'M SO over being pregnant.

Pregnant, bored, and homesick.

Declan does his best to put a smile on my face, and most of the time it works. But I'm so big now and I've still got six weeks to go.

"Are you okay?" Declan asks as he sits beside me on the couch. He wraps an arm around me. "Tell me what you need, sweetheart. It's all yours."

"I want to go home." I sniff.

"To LA? Let's go in the morning. It won't take long to pack, and ..."

I shake my head. "No. Home. I want my mum."

His expression softens. "Then, we'll do that."

"Really?" I bite my bottom lip.

"We can be on a plane tomorrow." Declan's mouth curls into a smile. "What's going on in that beautiful head of yours?"

"You really want to meet my parents?"

He throws his head back and roars with laughter. "I want to be with you. I'll have to meet them sometime. You need your mother, and I can deal with whatever your dad throws at me."

I snort. "You don't know what you're saying."

He drops to his knees in front of me. "I'd fight wars for you and this little one. He doesn't scare me."

Swallowing hard, I reach out and cup his cheek. "You're a good man. I hope you know that."

Declan shrugs. "I'm trying. I want to be better for you."

"You are being better. It's still so hard to reconcile how we met and how close we are now."

"Some things are meant to be." He pushes himself up and pecks me on the lips. "I'll call Joel and get him to check out some flights. Got your passport?"

"It's in my handbag."

"I'll grab it and make a call. One trip to New Zealand, coming right up."

He straightens himself up and I grasp his arm. "Thank you."

"Anything for you, Zoe. You should know that by now."

As he walks away, tears well in my eyes again. I'm not sure how he puts up with me being so emotional at times, but he's always level-headed. It's scary how in sync we are.

When he comes back into the room a few minutes later,

he's frowning a little, but as he sits beside me and wraps his arm around my shoulders, I know everything's okay.

"We're pushing it. We need to get a letter from the doctor to say you can travel, and if we're coming back here to have the baby we can't stay too long—two weeks at the most. Unless you want to have the baby there, in which case we'll need to find a midwife, and—"

"You got all that in a short conversation?"

"Joel's a walking encyclopaedia. If you call your doctor and get a letter emailed through, he can get us booked on the first flight out."

I just stare at him. It was only months ago that I was organised. Now I feel like I'm falling apart, and he's the one holding me together.

I call the doctor's office. We were only there a couple of days ago, so within a few hours, I have a letter saying I can fly and Joel has the tickets booked—with return tickets two weeks later.

It's not quite tomorrow, but in two days I'll be on a plane and on the way to see my parents.

My heart aches. I've missed them while I've been away, and I'm not sure how well my dad and Declan will get on given how close I am to my dad and Declan's wild ways, but I'm glad we're going.

TWENTY
DECLAN

A TRIP to New Zealand has always been on my bucket list.

But I just never got any offers to work down here.

Now I'm glad I'll see it for the first time with Zoe.

I moved heaven and earth to get us a flight out as soon as possible. She's got six weeks to go until her due date—too much later and we would never have been able to get on a plane.

We landed in Auckland a couple of hours ago, and now she's driving our rental car south to meet her parents. The scenery changes so quickly from the tall buildings of the city to the more famous rural landscape.

We could have flown to Taupo, but she wanted to drive, and we ended up flipping a coin over who would get behind the wheel. She wanted me to be free to enjoy the scenery, and although I would rather my heavily pregnant girl relax a bit more, I have to admit that it's wonderful to sit back as we pass those rolling hills.

"What the hell is this?" I point at the building made of corrugated iron in the shape of a dog. Next to it is a similar building, except it's a distinctive sheep shape.

We've been driving for two hours. I didn't think I'd end up hallucinating.

Zoe laughs. "That's the Tirau Visitor Centre."

I shoot her the side-eye. "Is it like this everywhere?"

"Well, there is a giant carrot in Ohakune, and then there's a big bottle of Lemon and Paeroa in Paeroa."

"What's a Paeroa?" Now I'm really confused.

"It's a drink named after the place. That's where it was originally made and the water in it came from there."

I nod as if this is making sense, but it's really not—although, that might also be because I'm tired. I'm not sure how Zoe has this much energy when she's this pregnant.

Maybe it's because she'll see her parents soon.

I haven't seen my parents in years. They never wanted me to be an actor—but I pushed so hard, and when my career took off in my teens, it wasn't long before that decision was taken out of their hands.

That was one strike. And then I was out of control, and they cut me off. I'm not sure I can salvage that relationship. It's been so long.

Instead, I'm focusing on Zoe and her parents. It means everything to me that I form a good relationship with them. It won't be easy—her mother and father are only ten years older than I am.

But then again, if Zoe was younger than her 30 years, I don't know if I'd be comfortable with our age gap. I was never one to chase much younger women, even though there was never a shortage of them throwing themselves at me.

"You're quiet," Zoe says.

"Just thinking about your parents and how *that's* going to go."

She reaches across the centre console and squeezes my hand. "You'll be fine. You'll charm my mother, and my dad's pretty easy-going."

"And you're his only daughter."

She pauses. "I am. But I've always been independent. I was out of there at eighteen and never really looked back. We're close, but they've always respected my decisions."

I nod slowly. "Makes sense. You and your app show you've got a good head on you."

Her smile lights up my heart

"Wait. Does that make you my sugar mamma?" I shrug.

Her laughter echoes through car, and we're soon through the small town of Tirau and back among the green hills. I could eat out on this feeling forever—making her happy.

I look out the window. We whiz past a sign welcoming us to Taupo, and she slows.

"So. We're here?"

She nods. "Yes, but we're going to McDonald's before we go home. I'm starving."

I'm not sure if that will help my nerves, but my girl is hungry, and I could do with something to eat. "That sounds good. I could kill a burger right now."

Thankfully there's no one waiting at the drive-through, and we have our food within minutes.

"Let's eat this by the lake," Zoe says.

She pulls into a park by the waterfront, and we walk the short distance to a bench where we sit.

"It's so beautiful." I stare out across the water. In the distance, on the other side of the lake sits three snow-covered peaks. It's cold, but Zoe prepared me well for the change of seasons.

"There's a giant volcano under the lake." Zoe leans her head on my shoulder. "A caldera."

"Like in *Yellowstone*?"

She nods. "The story goes that if the water in the lake warms up, you get the hell out of town."

"And the other mountains?"

Zoe points into the distance. "That's Ruapehu, Ngauruhoe, and Tongariro. All volcanoes."

I turn my head to look at her. "Where have you brought me?"

She laughs. "You're safe."

I take a bite of my burger and moan. "I didn't realise just how much I needed this."

"Well, I figured we could take a breath before I introduce you to Mum and Dad." She takes a large bite and fixes her gaze on me while she chews.

"That bad, huh?" I smile.

She finishes chewing and swallows before swiping the corner of her mouth with her thumb. "Everything will be fine. It's just probably easier to deal with meeting new people on a full stomach." After reaching for a fry, she sucks it down before continuing. "Thank you for bringing me here. Even sitting by the water makes me feel better."

"I'd do anything for you."

She meets my gaze. I mean it. I would go to the ends of the earth for this woman, and given how far we've travelled, maybe I have.

It's not just that I love her. Being with Zoe settles me in a way that I've not known before. She's so calm and level-headed, and she makes me feel the same.

We eat in silence, the cool breeze coming off the lake waking me up after our long flight and drive.

"We should go and do this," she says.

"You almost sound like you don't want to."

Zoe loops her arm in mine and leans her head on my shoulder. "It's just so peaceful here. I love that I get to share this with you."

I plant a kiss on the top of her head. "I do too. I'd rather be here with you than anywhere else in the world."

"Even if you're about to meet my father?"

I smile. "Even then."

She sighs before pushing herself to her feet. I gather our wrappers and put everything in a nearby garbage can.

"Ready?" I ask her, slipping an arm around her shoulders.

"Are you?"

Laughing as we walk toward the car, I nod. "I'm ready for anything."

"Come on then."

It's a short drive to her parents' house, and we soon pull down a driveway and into a backyard. A large garage sits on the other side of the yard, and a couple—I presume her parents—are out tending the garden. It's a warm, sunny day, and they have both flowers and vegetables growing along the fence.

This is Zoe's family home—the one she grew up in. They've been here her whole life, even though she wanted to buy them a new home when she sold her business.

I draw in a deep breath as she reaches across and squeezes my arm, and then I get out of the car, round it, and open her door.

She takes my hand and rises from her seat, giving me a reassuring smile.

"Zoe." Her mother walks toward us, her face lit with excitement.

"Mum." Zoe's voice cracks and she walks around the front of the car and straight into her mother's arms. "Declan, this is my mother, Serena."

"It's so good to meet you, Declan." Serena smiles at me.

Her father's right behind her.

"So this is him?" he asks.

He grunts and holds out his hand. "Brian Drake."

I grasp his hand and give it a firm shake. "Declan O'Leary."

Brian nods. "Heard a lot about you." We've not spoken before—I think Zoe's kept a distance between us until we could meet in person.

"All good, I hope." I know I'm baiting him. Her parents have the Internet. He'll have looked me up.

He tilts his head. "Zoe's happy and that's what matters to me."

She very clearly has a close relationship with her parents —one I can't relate to.

But I hope I can forge a good relationship with them.

I have to, for Zoe's sake.

TWENTY-ONE
DECLAN

IT'S BEEN years since I've felt so at peace.

We've spent the past two weeks with Zoe's parents, and she's relished her time here. It's been hard to find time to be intimate, but I do at least get to sleep with her in my arms.

Although she's more and more restless at night, finding it harder to rest.

We have to make a decision and soon about where we're having this baby. All her care has been in the US to date, but if she chooses to stay here, then we'll need to start making new arrangements.

Things have been amicable with Zoe's parents. Her mother's lovely and welcoming, but her father's kept his distance. Knowing our trip here may be coming to an end, it's time to ask him the question that's been burning in my gut since we arrived here.

Something changed in me the minute Zoe told me she was pregnant. She had no reason to trust me given my past, but she let me in, and she's changed my life. It's not just about the pregnancy anymore.

I want to spend the rest of my life loving her.

And I want to do this properly, which means swallowing any fear and talking to her father. I doubt he'll be happy if I whisk her away and marry her without his approval. He's seen how devoted I am to her, and I can only hope that stands me in good stead with him.

He's in his beloved garden again when I find him. His smile is tight, as every smile he's given me since I've arrived has been.

"Brian? I wondered if I could have a word."

He gives me a short, sharp nod.

"I'll be talking to Zoe today about her choice where to have the baby. I've told her I don't mind which country, but if we're going back to the US, we'll have to go back now before she can't travel. So, I wanted to talk to you about our future."

His right eye twitches. "Your future."

"I want to spend the rest of my life with her. If she'll have me."

He frowns and drops his gaze to the ground a moment before fixing it back on me. "I'm not sure I like you, but I also don't know you. What I do know is that you're closer to my age than you are my daughter's, and that makes me uncomfortable."

I nod. "I understand."

He pauses, grounding the toe of his show in the gravel. "She's also a grown woman who makes her own decisions. And I see the way you take care of her. If she's happy, then I'm happy. But I warn you, if you hurt her, you'll have me to answer to." His gaze hits mine—that intense blue he shares with Zoe, and I nod again.

"I'll always do my best to protect her. And our child."

"Her mother and I miss her. Zoe always was too independent for our liking." He chuckles. "But she went out and made a name for herself, and we couldn't be more proud. It's hard to let go."

I grip his shoulder. "I swear to you that I'll do right by her."

He nods slowly. "Just be sure you do. She's got a big heart, and if you break it, I'll come after you."

"I'd expect nothing less." I pause and brace myself. "I'm glad we're here. I want to marry your daughter. She has no idea yet—the pregnancy has been hard on her, but if she wants me, I'll spend the rest of my life making her happy."

His brows twitch. "Can you do that?"

I hold up my palms. "I know I don't have the best track record, but the past few months have been amazing, and I'd already decided to make changes in my life before she fell pregnant. I'm retired from movies, and I just want to settle down with Zoe and our child."

He swallows hard, his Adam's apple bobbing.

"I also know I don't need your blessing, but I'd like it."

"I'm not sure I can give it—not yet anyway. I hope you can respect that."

Shit. That's a blow, but not an unexpected one. "Then I hope I can prove I'm worthy of it."

Brian shakes his head. "Look, Declan. I don't know if I'd approve of *any* man that Zoe ended up with. She's that special to me. But I'm prepared to try if you will. I'll let you know when you have my blessing."

"That's all I can ask for."

After we've finished talking, I head inside and to Zoe's room where she's been napping. She sits on the end of the bed and looks up as I walk in.

"Everything okay?" Her brow is furrowed in concern, and I love her for it. It's clear it means a lot to her that I get on with her parents, and while there are a ton of reasons for them not to want me anywhere near her, they've been nothing but fair to me. It's been a long time since I've felt like part of any family.

"Everything is great." I sit beside her and slide my arm around her waist. "Are you okay? Have you enjoyed your stay here?"

"It's always good to be back home." She sighs. "But then this isn't home anymore. If you know what I mean."

I chuckle. "I think so. But to me, anywhere you are is home."

Her lips twitch. "That's so cheesy, but I get it. I feel the same way about you."

"Do you ... want to go back home to the States?"

She beams her brilliant smile at me. "I would love to go home with you, Mr O'Leary."

I run my hand across her belly. "I'm glad you're feeling better. Now all that's left to do is to wait for this one to arrive."

"I can't wait."

I pull her toward me and kiss her temple. "Neither can I, sweetheart. Neither can I."

TWENTY-TWO
ZOE

I'M NOT sure what's going on.

We've been back a few days, and Declan has been on his phone for what feels like hours at a time. And he's not talking to me.

I know he's spoken to Josh—I've heard his name come up once or twice as he's walked into the kitchen to make more coffee.

It's bugging me that he's being so secretive about it.

"We need to talk."

My stomach sinks when he walks toward me, a cautious smile on his face and his hands clasped together.

Is this it? Has he decided that his career is the most important thing after all? What will happen to me? Us?

"What's going on?"

He reaches for me, taking my hand in his. "Josh Carter's offered me a movie role. A big one."

I search his eyes. He's not giving me any sign as to how

he's feeling about this. Is he happy? Excited? Unsure what I'll think? "What kind of role?"

"One of the leads in an action film he's producing. I don't have all the details, but he wants to give me a chance to rebuild my career."

I turn, walk to the couch and drop onto it.

Declan sits beside me and pulls me into his arms. "It's been a while since I had an opportunity like this. He called me before Nikki because he knows Nikki will pile on the pressure to do it."

"And this way you get a chance to think about it."

He nods.

The last thing I want to do is push him away now. Do I like this? I'm not sure. His past is littered with moments where he's gone off the rails, and that always seems to happen with him after a shoot. I'm not sure I could cope if that happened. But at the same time, I have to have faith in him.

"Maybe you should consider his offer."

Declan scans my expression. "You really think so? I've found what I've been looking for." He runs his hand across my baby bump. "You and this little one. You're all I need."

I chew my bottom lip. Are we really enough to keep him happy? I'd like to think so, but something keeps nagging me that he has unfinished business. And who wants to go out of their career on a low?

"You don't think that's true?" he asks.

Pausing for a moment, I draw in a breath. "It's just ..." I squeeze his bicep. "You're amazing. You've been in all these wonderful movies, and I know that there have been a lot of ups and downs."

His lips quirk. "That's an understatement."

"Are you worried you won't be able to keep your word about drinking?"

His gaze drops, and he nods. "Taking time away has really cleared my head. I worry about the temptation of it all. I don't want to drink again."

"Then don't." I shift a little so I'm closer to him. "If you work with Josh, you'll be surrounded by people who don't want you to go down that track. And I'll be there too."

His eyes meet mine. "You will?"

"There's nothing stopping us from moving to LA. We can both be with you the whole way."

His smile grows. "You'd do that? I thought you were considering going back to New Zealand."

"Things have changed a lot since we had that conversation. We'll be a family. I have a few ideas about things I can work on next, but there's no rush. And there's no reason why I can't do that from home or wherever you're filming."

He leans over and kisses me tenderly. "I do love the idea of coming home to you."

"I'm not telling you to do it, Declan. But I will be there beside you all the way if you do." I run my finger up his arm. "Something tells me you've got unfinished business, and you've just found the right support crew to help you."

He's torn. I can see it all over his face. But I know a thing or two about unfinished business, and while I'm more than happy to just disappear with him and live our life together, I don't want him to feel like there's something missing.

"Talk to Josh." I press a palm to his chest. "See what he has to offer. I don't want you to live with regrets."

"Whether I do it or not, I have zero regrets. I have you."

"Sweet talker." I smile.

"I love being with you, do you know that? I can be open and honest, and I know I'll get that in return."

My heart swells. Our relationship has gone beyond sex and even love. It's a true partnership, one I never envisioned when Declan moved in with me.

We're working together and it feels so good.

This isn't going to be easy—trusting him not to fall back into bad habits is an exercise in patience.

But if he knows I have faith in him, maybe that will give him the extra incentive to succeed.

Won't it?

TWENTY-THREE
DECLAN

CAN I REALLY DO THIS?

It was only a half a year ago that I was prepared to walk away completely, but Josh's offer plagues me.

I've been given a chance to start my life again thanks to Zoe, but am I always going to wonder what might have been if I say no?

One thing is for sure—I don't deserve Zoe and all the good she brings to my life, but now she's here, the last thing I want to do is let her down.

"Declan."

"Hi, Josh."

His tone is warm. "I'm so glad you called. Have you given any thought to my offer?"

I scratch the back of my neck. "It's been hard to think about anything else."

He chuckles. "I doubt that. You're about to have a baby. I know what that's like."

I can't help but grin. While I don't know Josh well, I can tell he's a decent guy, and a family man to boot. I really hope that we can become friends no matter what my decision is. He's the type of person I need to be around—someone who's down to earth.

"There's not long to go now. I'm not sure how Zoe puts up with me."

That just makes Josh laugh harder. "I get it. When we had Addison, I don't know who was more excited. Poor Delaney had to deal with all those pregnancy issues while all I could think about was holding my little girl."

"That sounds like us. I can't wait to be a dad."

"It's life-changing." He pauses. "So, what do you think about this movie? Any questions?"

"No, it's just ... I'm still thinking about it. Zoe's given me the go-ahead, but I have to be sure."

"I know about your past." He pauses. "Worried you'll fall back into old habits?"

My throat tightens. He's hit the nail on the head. These past few months with Zoe have been everything.

"I'm not sure I can risk it."

He sighs. "Look, Declan. If the answer's no, then it's no. For what it's worth, I understand. My family is everything to me. I'd walk away rather than lose Delaney and my girls. Whatever you decide, it's good with me. But we do start shooting early next year, and I don't have a leading man."

"I understand. I'll have an answer for you really soon."

"This life is crazy. I never went down that path, but I do understand the temptations. Delaney was what kept me on the straight and narrow, even when we weren't together. That and good friends. And I hope whatever happens, we can be that."

I grin. "Zoe's bestie will flip if I tell her I'm friends with you."

Josh laughs. "Give me a call any time you need anything. Or Reece. We're here for you and Zoe. Hell, Delaney would love to spend more time with her. She collects other New Zealanders."

"I hope you mean that figuratively." I chuckle.

"She likes taking Hollywood newbies under her wing. It didn't take her long to become a pro at handling all the crazy stuff. I lucked out, and I think you did too from the sounds of it."

Zoe's given me the go-ahead. Josh and his crowd are supportive.

I can do this.

"I really did." I close my eyes for a moment and take a deep breath. "I want this movie. I want to work with you. I want my career back."

"I'm glad to hear it. What made up your mind?"

I swallow hard. "I feel like I have people on my side. Maybe that's what I needed. I mean, I've always had my manager, but Zoe says Delaney said something when we saw you that's been on my mind."

"Oh?"

"She said that no one in your group had family here so you made your own village. I want that for me and for Zoe."

He blows out a breath. "That sounds like Delaney. And it's true. If you're in LA, we will welcome you with open arms. Zoe won't be alone. I can guarantee that. And you won't either. We'll give you any support you need."

My voice cracks. "That sounds great."

"Welcome to the family, Declan. You won't regret it. I'll get a contract over to your manager and you, and we'll take it from there."

I punch the air. Making the decision takes a huge weight off my shoulders. Whatever happens, in LA Zoe will have people around her and the support she doesn't have in San Francisco. And I have her and our child.

Maybe this time I can have everything.

TWENTY-FOUR
ZOE

IT'S EARLY one evening when our child decides it's time to evict herself.

Declan catches on pretty quickly as we're curled up in front of the television watching one of his old movies.

"Are you timing those contractions?" he asks.

"How did you know I was having contractions?" I ask.

He leans in and nuzzles my cheek. "The way you suck in your breath. They're about ten minutes apart."

I bite my lip. "I wasn't going to say anything yet. I've been trying to stay calm."

"Because you think I'm going to freak out?"

"Maybe?" I tear up, and he brushes my cheeks with his fingers.

"What's going on?"

My lips twitch while I think of an answer. Because I don't know what's going on. I've been on a roller coaster of emotions for months. I'm not sure why the idea of being in labour is making me a nervous wreck.

"The baby's coming," I whisper.

He wraps his arm around my shoulders. "Let's call the doctor and check in with her."

One phone call later, with the contractions increasing, we leave for the hospital. I'm a hot mess by the time we make it to the delivery room. And the very first nurse who does a double take at Declan gets a taste of my wrath.

"Don't look at him," I yell.

Declan squeezes my hand. "Sweetheart—"

"Don't you sweetheart me, Declan O'Leary. I hate it when other women look at you."

He clamps his lips together.

"I'm so sorry," the nurse says.

Declan stands and presses a kiss to my temple. "It's okay. Zoe just gets … territorial."

I slap his chest. "Don't speak for me."

"I'm sorry, my love. I'm trying my best to take care of you."

I whimper as the pain begins to build again. "Am I really your love?"

He presses his forehead to mine. "Always. I love you, Zoe. Please can you park the jealousy until after you've got our baby in your arms?"

"I want my baby."

"I know. I can't wait to meet them too."

This baby's not co-operated once during scans. It's not that we didn't want to know the gender—we never got a chance to find out.

Something tells me Declan's right when he says he thinks we're having a girl. This baby's stubborn like me.

For the next few hours, he doesn't put a foot wrong. He feeds me ice chips and rubs my back when I need it. And he's completely focused on me.

A little after midnight and after an hour of pushing, our daughter makes her appearance. It's love at first sight. She's got a shock of dark hair and dark eyes like her father. In fact, there's no denying she's Declan's daughter as she has his chin too. Declan's in tears as he cuts the cord.

I've never been so overwhelmed with emotion and exhaustion. I want to hold and nurse her all night, but I also want to collapse and sleep for the next week.

We already made arrangements for Declan to stay in hospital with me—I don't know if I could cope if he had to go home. I just want him and our daughter close.

"What are we going to call her?" I ask.

He chuckles. "We should have talked about this."

"We were too busy with other things."

I close my eyes as Declan places a soft kiss on my cheek. "I think you should name her. You did all the work."

Stroking my daughter's fuzzy little head, I sigh. "How about Daisy Grace? I always liked Daisy as a name, and Grace is my mother's middle name."

"Daisy Grace. My girl." Declan's voice shakes a little as he wraps his arms around us. My heart's never been so full of love. For our daughter. For him.

It scares the hell out of me.

My biggest fear is that we'll just be a flash in the pan for him. I think back to where this all started—when I confidently told him I didn't need him. That might have felt true then, but everything's changed. What if he ditches us for the life he had before?

"I'll buy a house," he says.

Panic rises in me. "What? Where?"

He tilts his head. "Wherever you are. Where else?"

Tears well in my eyes as I take in his announcement. We've grown so close—been intimate while I've been pregnant. Is our daughter about to live between two homes? Aren't we enough to keep him near?

"Maybe four bedrooms. Nothing too big. Enough room for us and our little one with room to grow in case we decide to have more children. And a garden for them to play in. That's important. We don't need that big house."

I let out a sob in relief, and he fixes his gaze on me. "Zoe? Are you okay? Are you in pain?"

Shaking my head, I swipe away the tears from my cheeks. "I thought ... I thought you were moving out."

"Without you?"

I nod.

Declan gathers me in his arms and strokes my back. I breathe in the reassuring scent of *him*. All these months together and I didn't want to fall in love, but it's far too late for that.

"I'm not going anywhere without you. Or our daughter. We're a family now. I love you, Zoe Drake."

I sniff. "I love you too. And don't sell your other house. I love it too much."

He chuckles. "Me too, but don't you think it's a bit too big?"

"It's perfect. The bathtub is perfect."

His chuckle turns to a roar of laughter. "You want to keep the house because of the bathtub?"

"Yes. And maybe it's big, but we can make it a home. And I know you love it."

He grins. "If it makes you happy, then that's what we do."

I breathe out a long sigh. "I'll miss San Francisco, but with Caitlin married and living somewhere else, there's nothing for me here. But your life is in LA, and we'll be there while you're filming anyway …"

Declan nods. "Makes sense."

"And with that big house, I don't want Daisy growing up alone. I know we haven't talked about the future, but …"

"I'll give you as many babies as you want." He kisses me softly. "There's nothing I wouldn't do for you, Zoe."

TWENTY-FIVE
DECLAN

I STEP out of my trailer and take a deep breath.

I've never been nervous on set before—or maybe I was years ago, but those days are a bit of a blur from the excitement I'd felt at the time.

I'm not just out to re-establish my name. I want to impress Josh—his career followed a similar path to mine, but he got everything right, and I want Zoe to be proud of me.

She and Daisy are my whole world now.

I know this is an ego project—but it could also be the start of something new. A career without the baggage of the past. A fresh start. There's no giving in to temptation ever.

While I used to have a hip flask in my trailer no matter what I worked on, there's no alcohol at all on set now.

Not that I would risk my family for anything.

My past is behind me, and it's up to me to make sure it stays there. What I have with Zoe is so grounding that I've come to realise how I wasn't ready for my first two marriages.

I was too young when I married Ciara—I should have worked out who I was before I committed.

And the less said about my marriage to Annabelle, the better.

My future is brighter than it's ever been—whether I ever work again or not.

"Hi, Declan." Hadley Bridger saunters toward me. She's an up-and-coming actress who's one of my co-stars in this movie—the one I have a sex scene with. I've seen some of her work—she's talented, but right now I have a sinking feeling in my gut as she twirls a lock of blonde hair around her finger and crosses her high-heeled feet when she comes to a stop.

"Hadley."

"So, we'll be working together."

I'm not sure I can remember her voice being so husky on the audition tape I saw, and I raise an eyebrow. "It seems so."

Despite my wild ways in the past, I never hooked up with anyone on set. Even I drew limits on my behaviour when it came to being *that* unprofessional.

"I wondered if you might want to join me for a drink in my trailer."

Maybe I never got entangled with a co-star, but I have been known to share a drink with one.

Zoe deserves better.

It's tempting—the drink, not the woman, but I know what I have waiting for me at home.

"Ahh, darlin', you don't want to mess up your career like I did. Stay off the drink. Don't do drugs," I say.

Her expression drops. "I thought …"

"I'm sober and plan on staying that way. I've just become a father, and that means more to me than any drink ever will."

She falters but recovers quickly. "You could still visit me in my trailer …"

I shake my head. "Thanks for the invite, but I'll be sticking to my own."

"Declan."

Turning toward the sound of the very welcome voice, I grin. "Josh. I didn't know you'd be coming to set."

He beams, holding out his hand, and I shake it. "Had to be here for the first day. To be honest, you'll see me a lot. Reece and I are very involved in all our productions." He nods toward Hadley. "Hadley, it's good to see you again."

"Oh, you too." She flutters her eyelashes, and I bite down a smile.

"How's Delaney?" I ask Josh.

His eyes light up. "She's good. Been asking after Zoe. We'll have to get together one weekend now you're back here. I'll give you Delaney's number and maybe Zoe can give her a call?"

I fist-bump him. "That'd be great. Zoe's climbing the walls a bit and still settling in."

He chuckles. "Oh, I can just see Delaney and her friends helping her. I assume the baby's keeping you busy."

"She's sleeping well, but Zoe's tired."

Josh claps me on the shoulder. "She needs support. We'll sort that out."

"Thanks, Josh."

"You're part of our family now."

His words warm my heart. All this time, I never thought

I'd be a part of anything—I've always been a bit of a lone wolf. But now, no matter what, I've found friends.

And best of all, Zoe has too.

THE HOUSE ECHOES with baby cries, and I sigh as I walk into the living room.

Where are they?

I follow the sound until I reach the kitchen where Zoe paces back and forward, patting Daisy's back. Her eyes are closed, and it's clear she hasn't had a good day.

"Babe? You okay?"

Her eyes flick open. "I think she just needs to burp, but it's not happening."

"Let me take her. You lie down."

She shakes her head. "I'm fine."

"You're exhausted. I can see that. I'll take care of her, and you go and have a soak in the bath and a sleep."

"You've been working too."

I roll my eyes. "Oh, please. It was the first day on set and just a big meet-and-greet. You're doing the hard stuff. Did you feed her?"

Daisy wails and Zoe's lower lip wobbles. "Yes, she's been fed," she whispers.

"Well, that gives you a few hours. Let me do my thing." I lean over and kiss her softly, reaching for the baby. Once I've got her in my arms, I nod toward Zoe. "Get out of here."

She's struggling to smile—it's obvious, and I don't take my

eyes off her as she walks out of the living room toward the stairs.

I know what she's like. She'll be having a bath with one ear tuned in to listen for Daisy. If I can't get our girl to sleep, she'll be back and stressing again.

Moving Daisy to my shoulder, I cradle her head with one hand and rub her back with the other. "Come on, little one."

It takes a few minutes until a burp any grown man would be proud of erupts from my tiny daughter, and I grin. "That's my good girl."

The crying stops, and she whimpers as I carry her up the stairs and toward our room.

I smile at the splashing sound coming from the bathroom.

Sitting on the edge of the bed, I rock Daisy, her big dark eyes staring up at me.

"I'm your daddy, little one. Yes, I am." I'll never get enough of saying that. This little girl won't ever want for anything.

"Daisy, Daisy, give me your answer do," I croon. "I'm half-crazy all for the love of you."

Her tiny eyelids flutter, and she snuffles before they close.

Zoe needs support. All she has is me, and if I'm not here to help her out then times like earlier will be stressful to her. What more can I do to help?

I'm not sure how long I sit there, but soft footsteps behind me make me turn.

"She's asleep?" Zoe whispers.

I nod. "Once she got that air out, she was halfway there."

She frowns. "How do you do that? I'd been trying for half an hour."

Shrugging, I reach for her, and she sits on the bed beside me. She watches Daisy sleeping with a pout on her face—one I'm planning on removing.

"Magic touch, I guess. Let me put her in her crib and I'll show you."

Zoe tilts her head. "I think you're pushing your luck."

"I can be gentle."

She slaps my arm. "I thought you said I should rest. That's not resting."

"You don't have to do anything."

After standing, she then walks around the bed and drops her bathrobe to the floor. She's wearing sleep shorts and a satin tank top, her nipples prominent against the fabric.

I let out a low wolf whistle, and she blushes.

"Stop it."

"You're so beautiful, Zoe."

She holds up her palms. "I'm taking a nap while the baby's sleeping."

I place Daisy in her crib and tuck her in before turning back to the bed.

I strip down to my underwear then slide into bed beside Zoe. She sighs as I spoon her from behind.

"Declan, I ..."

"It's okay. I'm going to nap with you. I know you need sleep. When she wakes up, I'll get her."

Zoe wriggles out from beside me and rolls onto her back. She reaches for my face, cupping my cheek, and I lean in to kiss her softly.

"I'm sorry. I'm just so tired." She yawns.

"I love sex with you, but I'm never going to push it when I

can see how exhausted you are. Is there anything else I can do to help?"

She shrugs. "We just need to get into a proper routine. This moving around hasn't helped, but now we're here we can settle in properly."

"I'm sure I wasn't helping by being out of the house all day."

Zoe studies me for a moment. "You're doing what you have to do. I get that. And I know you'd be supportive if the shoe was on the other foot."

"You bet I will be."

Her smile is faint, her eyes heavy. "We'll work it all out. I love you."

"You're the best thing that ever happened to me, Zoe Drake. I thought my heart was dead until I met you. And now you and that little girl are the reason it beats every day."

She pats my cheek. "You make me happy too."

"I'll call Josh and see if we can round up some visitors. I know Delaney has been champing at the bit to see you."

"That would be nice." It's clear now she's fighting sleep, and she yawns and turns back over.

I snuggle in against her and close my eyes. These are the moments that make everything worth it.

TWENTY-SIX
ZOE

DECLAN IS as good as his word.

One call to Josh and the cavalry arrives.

Delaney is on my doorstep the next morning. She'd dropped one child to Lana's and the other was in school, so she is all mine for the day—or for however long I need her.

All I do is cry all over again.

I have a village.

Delaney, Pania, and Lana, spend the next few weeks swooping in and out and taking the pressure off me. Most times, it's just nice being able to sit and talk. Other times, they take care of Daisy while I get some sleep.

My confidence as a first-time mother grows as I get the help I need. At times I feel so useless, but Delaney tells me the story of how her mother kicked her out when she found out she was pregnant with Amelia, and how Pania and her mother stepped in to help.

"I couldn't have done it without my village," she says. And I have to agree with her. I could fly my parents over, but I'm also wary since mine and Declan's relationship is still fairly new, and living with my parents might not be the greatest idea. Besides, they both work and have responsibilities of their own. We've already planned to go and see them once Declan's movie shoot is over.

Declan has invited us down to the set today for lunch. I get the feeling he's as keen to show his daughter off as he is for me to see his workplace.

I drive in the gate and pull in where the security guard shows me. Declan walks toward the car, opens the boot, and pulls out the pram while I get Daisy out of her car seat.

"I'm so glad you're here. Josh is somewhere around today, and we just broke for lunch. Your timing is perfect."

I peck him on the lips, and he takes Daisy from my arms and lowers her into the pram. "I'm excited to look around. I've never been on a movie set before."

"It's not that exciting. But I can show you my trailer." His eyebrows waggle, and I laugh. This is the Declan I love—so relaxed and flirty with me. I'm glad he's working again if this is what he's like when he does.

We make our way toward a tented area where people are sitting at tables.

"The food trucks are just over here. It won't be anything too fancy, but there's a good selection of food. We'll eat and then I'll show you around."

"Declan? I was hoping we could run lines?"

I swallow hard. I swear the woman coming towards us is

making heart eyes at my partner. My jealousy isn't helped by the fact that she's gorgeous. Blonde shoulder-length curls surround a heart-shaped face with big blue eyes and rosebud red lips. *This is his co-star?*

In the haze of dealing with my newborn, I'd heard her name but never looked her up.

"Not today, Hadley," he replies, his voice smooth as silk.

"Oh?" She pouts. God, she even looks good when she does that. Is this what he's had in front of him daily for the past two weeks?

I push my feelings of inadequacy down, but Declan seems to pick up that something's wrong as he wraps his arm around my shoulders.

"My girls are here to spend some time with me."

Hadley's eyes flick to me, and it's like she barely registers my existence before they shift back to Declan. "So, you'll be around later?"

I exchange a glance with Declan. *What the hell?*

He shrugs. "Probably not. I'm meeting with the director this afternoon and then I'll be going home."

I've never felt so plain. Here's this beautiful woman, dressed to the nines, making a play for my man right in front of me. I'm wearing no makeup and stuffed into jeans that only just fit after giving birth two months ago.

I will not cry.

He's not giving her an inch, but this still hits me in ways I know it shouldn't. Where's my fight?

"Really? Please, Declan?" Hadley reaches out, placing her hand on his forearm.

Found it.

I draw in a deep breath. Declan shakes her hand off. "Yes. Really. You need to find someone else to run lines with. I've got better things to do."

He squeezes my arm and plants a kiss on my temple, and I breathe a sigh of relief.

"Oh, thank God. I thought I'd become invisible," I say.

She shifts her gaze to me. "Oh, are you Declan's girlfriend?" The way she says it, it's like she's spitting razor blades.

"Yes, I am. And you are?"

Her lips tremble—I've clearly hit a nerve. Am I supposed to know who she is?

"Zoe, this is Hadley. She's in the movie."

Not *'my co-star.'* Not anything more important than *'She's in the movie.'* I think this is Declan's way of putting her in her place.

"Now, if you'll excuse us, I'm taking my gorgeous girlfriend to lunch." He slides his hand into mine. "Have a good day, Hadley."

He takes over pushing the pram until we reach an empty picnic table, and Declan indicates I should sit.

"What's up with her?"

He shrugs. "She's new. This is her first big movie. I'm sure she's heard stories, but half the stuff out there about me isn't true. I might have had a few drinks while on set, but I never screwed the crew—or my co-stars."

My heart leaps. "She's gorgeous. She doesn't need to—"

"No, she doesn't. But either way, I'm not interested." He

takes my hand in his and runs his thumb across my knuckle. "Not when I have perfection at home."

My cheeks burn. We haven't had sex since Daisy's birth, and Declan has been nothing but patient. I just haven't felt comfortable in my own body.

"Anyway, are you hungry? I'll stay here with Daisy if you want to go and have a look and grab something. Then I'll go."

I nod. "Sounds good."

After making my way to the food trucks, I walk along, looking at the choices until I come to the lasagna. My mouth waters at the thought of pasta and cheese.

"Oh, that's way too many carbs for me." Hadley's right behind me and I bristle.

"Breastfeeding burns through *so* many calories." I smile.

She gives me a sharp nod.

Yeah, I've got a connection to Declan that no one else will ever have.

I take my plate and make my way back to our table, making sure to place a kiss on Declan's lips when I sit down.

"Go get some food. Don't eat too many carbs. Hadley doesn't approve."

His eyebrows nearly take off into orbit. "What?"

"It's okay. The way Daisy eats, I'll have burned this off by afternoon tea."

He chuckles and places a kiss on my temple as I raise my fork to take my first bite. "Love you."

"You too." I moan when I slide that first mouthful in. His eyes are on my lips as I chew and swallow. "God, that is to die for."

"Maybe I should invite you to lunch every day. I could just watch you eat."

I laugh and slap his arm softly. "Go and get your food."

He returns with his own plate of lasagna, and I look up to see Hadley watching us. It's sad. If that's the way she thinks she's going to get ahead, she's sorely mistaken.

Dark thoughts swirl in my head about Declan being tempted, but then I watch him and he only has eyes for our daughter, and then he turns them on me.

"Have you had a good day?" he asks.

I nod. "So far, so good. She was a bit fussy this morning, but she did one of those man burps and then smiled at me."

He chuckles. "That kid's got to be the biggest burper ever. That's *my* daughter."

I grin. "Only you would be proud of that."

"Thank you for coming to see me. It really does make my day." He leans over and pecks me on the lips. "If I had my way, I'd have you two here all the time with me."

"I think I'd go mad. At least at home I can watch the daytime soaps. And I get visitors."

He takes a bite of his lunch as he nods. "You know, movie aside, I think the best thing we could ever have done is make friends with Josh and his crowd. It's been good for you."

I scoop another generous mouthful onto my fork. "It has. They make me feel at home. The only person missing is Caitlin. I wish we got more time together."

He wraps one arm around my shoulders and pulls me closer. "We'll talk to her. Maybe she and Brandon can come and stay when it works in with his schedule. We've got plenty of room."

"I like that idea."

When we've finished lunch, he wraps his arms around me and kisses me hard—uncaring who sees. I love this man. I love that he's not afraid to show affection openly. It feels like he wouldn't mess around on me.

I trust him—I do, but I'm not sure I trust this environment.

In the meantime, he's done nothing wrong, so I have to have faith that his good behaviour will continue.

I'm not sure what the alternative would do to me.

BY MID-AFTERNOON, with Daisy out for the count, I'm bored.

I need to find a project, or to spend time online to find inspiration for my next business venture. Jason and Chrissie cut me off early and told me to take care of my baby, so I can't even log in to my old app and see what's happening there.

Being bored doesn't stop my wandering mind getting stuck on Declan and Hadley. The way she looked at him pissed me off.

My phone rings, and I smile as Delaney's name comes up.

"Hi, Delaney." She's been a regular visitor these past few weeks, but I haven't seen her in a couple of days. She always brings calm and cheer whenever she arrives.

"I was wondering if you were up for a visitor. I've just made some baby quiches, and—"

Delaney, I can talk to Delaney about this. She'll understand. She's got children and her husband's an actor.

"I'd love to see you," I blurt out.

"Are you okay?" she asks.

"I just really need to talk."

"I'm about ten minutes away," she says.

The crunch of tyres outside the front door alerts me to her presence a short time later. I fling open the door and smile at the sight of her carrying in a plastic container.

"I'll make some coffee. Come in."

Delaney follows me through to the kitchen where I get a couple of mugs and make coffee.

She goes to the cupboards and pulls out a plate before opening her container and placing the little quiches on it. "These are still warm."

"You're so good to me. Let's go into the living room."

With our food and coffee placed on the coffee table, I sit on the couch, and she catches my gaze, her eyes filled with concern.

"I know I asked you on the phone already, but are you okay? You sounded anxious."

I wring my hands together. "Can I ask you something personal?"

Delaney's brows twitch, but she nods. "Sure."

"How do you ... how do you deal with Josh doing sex scenes? Declan has one in this movie, and his co-star has hearts in her eyes, and ..."

Delaney lets out a sigh and drops onto the couch beside me, taking my hand in hers. "It's not easy. He always gives me a heads up if something's going to be in a movie, and I think if I pushed it, he just wouldn't do it. But I trust him, and the first time I saw him in a sex scene it was the hottest thing ever." Delaney fans herself with her free hand. "And now I'm good friends with the woman he filmed it with."

My eyes widen. "Really?"

"It was awkward at first. We'd just gotten back together, and then Josh was off filming. There were rumours about them. I didn't know Gabby then, but I'd seen her in movies. She's gorgeous."

I tilt my head. "*You're* gorgeous. And Josh obviously adores you."

She grins. "Thank you."

For a moment she pauses, and I take a sip of my coffee. "What's the rest of the story?"

Delaney's brows twitch. "Oh. There were photos of her going into Josh's trailer. And a story that talked up his new romance. I wanted to trust him so badly, but there was still that uncertainty."

My throat tightens. I don't think for a moment that Declan would put our relationship in danger. He loves me and adores our daughter.

Delaney places her hand over mine. "Zoe. He loves you. If you don't think you can handle it—tell him."

I chew my bottom lip.

"I let a misunderstanding keep Josh and I apart for six years when all we needed to do was communicate. Don't let that happen to you and Declan."

"You're right." I run my hand down my cheek. "I'll talk to him."

Delaney gives me a small smile. "It's not an easy life. But I'm always here to talk to, and so are the others. Anytime you need us, we're here for you."

I squeeze her arm. "Thank you. I'm so glad for you all."

Swallowing hard, I then blow out a breath. "It's just ... I thought I knew where my life was headed, and this past year it's all been turned upside down."

She nods. "I remember that feeling from when Josh and I got back together. From the media interest to people saying snarky stuff online—it's a lot to deal with. Plus, you had a baby not that long ago, and said goodbye to your work baby. You're amazing, Zoe. Don't ever forget that."

"Declan and I haven't had sex since Daisy," I blurt out. "I just feel so bloated and ..."

Her smile spreads. "He still thinks you're the hottest thing on two legs. None of us miss the way he looks at you."

"Really?"

She nods. "Like I said. Talk to him. He's probably waiting on you to give him the green light."

As if on cue, the baby monitor picks up Daisy's wail, and I make a move to stand.

Delaney pulls me back down. "I'll go and get her. You sit and take a break, Mamma. Gotta save that energy if you're having sex with the delectable Declan later." Shooting me a wink, she heads upstairs, returning moments later and rocking Daisy in her arms. "She's so beautiful. My ovaries are aching already."

I laugh. "Where's Addison?"

"With her father. Josh is home with me today, but I wanted to check on you because it's been a few days, and we're a pretty useless village if we don't keep in touch."

I hold out my arms and take an unsettled Daisy from her.

After unclipping my bra, I raise my top and put my baby to my breast where she latches on and feeds hungrily.

"I really appreciate everything you're doing. I'm not sure how I would have coped alone."

Delaney shakes her head. "Declan would have put everything on hold if you needed it. He spoke to Josh about his schedule to try and make it easier on you. That's how I know he loves you."

My heart swells. "He really does."

She sits on the couch and picks up her coffee. "I'm here whenever you need me. You know that. When she's old enough, I can even take her for a night to give you two time alone." I must grimace as she laughs. "I'm not talking any time soon," she continues.

"Thank you."

"You're always welcome."

DELANEY'S VISIT gave me a lot of food for thought.

I'm ready to have sex with Declan again—I know he'll be gentle and loving. It's my own insecurities coming into play and stopping me. And they're amplified by his return to acting, especially in a role where he'll have a love scene.

But I'm the one he loves.

I'm the one he wants.

He's even sexier to me now he's a father. The nights where he cradles Daisy and sings to her as we both try and get her to sleep are the best. He never shirks any responsibility when it comes to her—he's dealt with some of the worst nappies a breastfed baby can produce.

We're a family, and he's not giving that up.

I'm lost in thought when the front door closes, and I jump at the sudden sound.

Declan kisses the nape of my neck and rubs his nose up to my ear. "Did my girls have a good day?"

"We did. She's sleeping now. It's better now you're home, though."

He turns me around and scans my expression. "Are you okay, Zoe?"

"No, just feeling a little insecure."

He frowns, and wraps his arms over my shoulders. I close my eyes as he tightens his embrace. "Insecure about what?"

"If I'm not happy about my own body, why would you be? And then you're on set with that gorgeous woman who's very obviously interested in you."

He lets out a frustrated sigh and plants a kiss on my neck before loosening his grip. "I love *you*, Zoe Drake. I'm not going to risk my relationship with you for anything or anyone. What I am going to do is marry you."

My throat tightens. "Really?"

"That's the plan. I've just been putting off asking because I didn't know if you'd say yes, and the thought of you refusing me terrifies me."

I wriggle in his grasp until he lets me go. "Why?"

"I can handle just about anything right now, but being rejected by you might just kill me."

"Declan," I whisper.

"Look at us. We're such a pair. You feeling insecure

because of my job and me knowing I'm punching above my weight being with you and worried you'll say no if I ask you to marry me."

I blink rapidly. "You are?"

"Baby, you're all I've dreamed about since the day we met. I spent those weeks until you called me picking up the phone and putting it down dozens of times because I knew I wasn't good enough for you."

Tears roll down my cheeks. "I was hurt you didn't call."

"I'm a fool."

"I love you," I whisper.

"I can't imagine my life without you. When this movie is done, so am I. I'm really retiring this time."

When I shake my head, he grasps my chin and raises my gaze to meet his.

"I am, Zoe. There's no way I'm doing this to you, and I'll be going out on a high. It's so much better than that shitty movie I was last in."

"But—"

"No buts. I'm enjoying being back on set, but I can't do this again. Maybe Josh can find me another job doing something else behind the scenes, but I'd also be happy being a house husband if you wanted to spread your wings." My eyes widen, and he pecks me on the lips. "I meant work wise. You said you had to wait out your contract before starting any new projects. I want you to have the freedom to do that ... if you want to."

I throw my arms around his neck. It's so crazy to me that in what feels like a few short months, I've gone from feeling the loss of my best friend's presence and the loneliness that came with that to having the best, most supportive partner on the planet.

"Take me to bed."

He chuckles. "Now?"

"Daisy's asleep. There's no time like the present."

His face lights up. "Are you really ready? I don't want you to push yourself."

"We've both waited long enough." I drop my arms and slide my hand into his. "Please?"

"You don't have to ask twice, Zoe."

I laugh as he bends and throws me over his shoulder. He's careful on the stairs, but once we get to the bedroom, he unceremoniously dumps me on the bed, all while I giggle.

"I love the sound of your laughter," he says.

Propping myself up on my elbows, I raise my brows. "Is that all you love?"

"I love the taste of your pussy, too, which is what I'm about to help myself to." He reaches for the button of my jeans, and I groan with relief as he releases the tightness around my waist and tugs my pants down.

"Why are you wearing those when you're obviously uncomfortable?" he asks.

"I was just so happy to fit them again."

Declan shakes his head. "Don't push yourself. I want you to be happy—not squash your organs in some crazy effort to ... I'm not sure what you were doing."

"Feeling normal."

"Babe, you're not even two months post-partum. I know you want to push yourself, but I hate seeing you like this." He leans closer. "Besides, if you wear a dress or a skirt, I have much easier access to your pussy."

I lick my lips. "I guess you have a point."

"You know I do."

"Declan?"

"Zoe?"

"Just love me."

His expression softens. "That's the easiest thing in the world to do."

TWENTY-SEVEN
DECLAN

ONCE THE MOVIE IS WRAPPED, Zoe, Daisy, and I get on a plane and fly to New Zealand.

Zoe's parents have yet to meet Daisy—in person at least, and now I really am retired, I have all the time in the world.

At some point I'll have to do some promo work for the movie, but that's it. Unless there's a special reason for me to show my face in public, I really am done this time.

And I couldn't be happier.

It's a little extreme to fly a baby first class, but my girls are getting the best of everything from now on.

This time, there's no sign of Zoe's parents in the yard, but as soon as the car comes to a stop, the back door of the house bursts open and Serena runs toward the car.

Zoe opens her door and gets out, embracing her mother while I get Daisy's capsule out.

"Where is she?" Serena asks.

"Right here." I say.

She rounds the car and clasps her hands together. "Oh, she's so precious."

"Why don't we all get inside, Mum?" Zoe smiles.

"Of course. I'll make coffee. And then cuddles with the baby. How was your flight?"

"It was fine. Daisy slept for a lot of it, so I'm not sure how tonight will go."

They chatter as they walk into the house, and I trail along behind them.

"That was your grandmother, little one. Now to see if your grandfather likes me better than last time."

Daisy stares at me.

"I think you're the key to my full acceptance. Not going to lie—I'm going to use you to maximum effect."

She beams a brilliant toothless smile at me as if she knows what I'm saying. *Yeah, we're a team.*

"I'd high-five you if you were old enough to understand what Daddy's doing." I wink at her, and she keeps on smiling at me.

Taking a deep breath, I walk into the living room.

"Declan." Brian holds out his hand, and I give it a firm shake. "It's good to see you."

"I almost believe that, Brian." I chuckle.

He grins. "I'm glad you're all here. I can't wait to meet my granddaughter."

"She's amazing. I'll get her out of her capsule and you can hold her."

"Let's catch up. How long are you staying?"

I shrug. "For as long as Zoe needs to."

He laughs. "Good answer."

This is nice. The atmosphere is much different this time. I place the capsule on the floor and unclip Daisy's harness. After lifting her gently, I rock her before I place her into her grandfather's arms.

Brian's facade cracks, and his eyes give away how emotional he is as he breathes her in.

"Aren't you beautiful?" he says, his Adam's apple bobbing as he swallows hard. "Thank you, Declan."

"She and her mother are everything."

He meets my gaze and nods in understanding.

"Dad. What do you think? She seem to be taking after Declan so far." Zoe places a hand on my arm and leans her head on my shoulder.

"You did well." He beams with pride. "Oh, she smiled at me."

Zoe squeezes my bicep, and I press a kiss to the side of her head.

Brian makes his way to his recliner chair and sits, cradling Daisy and talking to her the whole way.

"Here's coffee and some biscuits. Let me know if you want anything more to eat." Serena comes into the room with a tray and places it on the table. Her eyes light up. "Oh, Brian. She's beautiful."

"Isn't she? Look at that smile."

I share a glance with Zoe. We stopped along the way when Daisy grizzled and made sure she was fed and changed before we got here. Brian and Serena wouldn't have cared, but we wanted her to be happy when she arrived.

She's a content baby. Once we got past those first few weeks, she became a lot more chill. She doesn't always sleep well, but we figure it's a matter of time before she settles down and with our village around us, we don't have to stress too much about how we'll make it work then. Zoe's taken to life in LA like a fish to water with the help of our friends.

We sit on the couch together and take in the sight of our daughter meeting her grandparents. It gives me pangs of sadness thinking how much my parents will miss, but I've got enough in my life. Maybe I'll send them some photos of their granddaughter, but their disowning me still stings.

I slip my arm around Zoe's shoulders, leaning back on the couch.

She smiles at me. "You okay?"

"Yeah. I really am."

Zoe snuggles into my side, and I kiss her temple.

Serena takes Daisy in her arms and rocks her while Brian fixes his gaze on us. He even smiles a little before reaching for his coffee cup and taking a sip.

It's amazing the difference a baby has made.

AFTER DINNER, I head outside for some fresh air.

Maybe we'll buy a house here—divide our time between Taupo and LA. Zoe would be keen, I'm sure of it.

"Beer?" Brian approaches me from behind, holding two bottles. "It's alcohol-free."

I nod. "Sure."

"I got them in especially when I knew you were coming." He takes a sip of his and hands me the other bottle. "They're not too bad."

"I'll give it a go." I take the bottle and look at the label. I've had Heineken before, but not the alcohol free.

"So you've retired again, I hear."

I nod. "I'm done with that life. It's nothing compared to being home with Zoe and Daisy."

"Why did you even make that movie if you were going to walk away?"

I pause. "I don't really know. Ego in part. My career had been going in the wrong direction for a long time, and I really thought it was over. But I got a great offer from a good man, and I took it." I meet his gaze. "If Zoe hadn't supported me, I would have turned it down. And then I knew after only a few days on set that it would be my last movie. I love your daughter, Brian, and I just want to be with her."

He studies me closely. "You gonna stick to retirement or change your mind again?"

I shake my head and smile. "It's not me anymore. Like I said, it didn't take me long to realise that. But I wanted my career to end on a high, and it will, which is better than the alternative. I want Zoe to be free to do whatever she wants whether that's being at home with Daisy too or creating another app or business."

He fights a smile—I can tell by the way his eyes twinkle—and I know I've said the right thing.

"Look." I press my palms together. "I know you're concerned about my relationship with Zoe. And you have every right to be. I'm not son-in-law material. But I'm trying to be a better man, and it's all because of her. She's given me a gift that I won't take for granted. Becoming a father has changed my life."

His jaw stiffens, as if he's trying to suppress his own emotion. But I'm done hiding behind any kind of masculine firewall. Zoe danced her way into my life and turned it upside down. And I wouldn't change a second of it.

"I understand," he finally says. "We were ... younger when we had Zoe, but that little girl made me want to work hard. I wanted to make sure her and her mother were taken care of. If I could have, I would have wrapped them both in bubble wrap so the world could never hurt them."

I chuckle. "I get what you mean."

"And then my little girl grew up and met you. I've googled you, you know. You've done some stupid stuff in your life. But you're good to Zoe, and Lord knows I can't tell her what to do anymore." He shifts his gaze away and draws a deep breath. "Last time you were here, you asked for my blessing. And I was reluctant."

"I understood. But I love her. Everything's easy when it comes to Zoe."

A smile shifts his lips. "I can't stop you from marrying my daughter. She's old enough to make up her own mind. We won't stand in your way, Declan. You have my blessing."

"I hope you know how much this means to me."

He nods. "I can see. And I see how you dote on Zoe. Keep that up, and you'll always have our support."

"Thank you."

He holds up his bottle. "To Daisy. You two have done well."

I clink my bottle with his. "Thank you again."

Brian points me toward the outdoor chairs. "Why don't we sit and talk? Get to know each other properly this time."

"That sounds great to me."

IN THE EVENING, when Daisy's asleep and Zoe's parents are watching TV, I walk into Zoe's bedroom where she's already in bed.

She looks up as I enter. "Are you okay?"

After stripping off, I slip into bed beside her, spooning her from behind. I kiss her neck and nuzzle behind her ear. "I am better than okay."

"Being here agrees with you too, huh?"

"Your father gave me his blessing," I whisper.

She rolls over, one eyebrow arched. "His blessing?"

I take her hand in mine. "I know this isn't the most romantic of places, but I can't wait any longer. I love you. I'm *in* love with you. You changed my life in the most amazing of ways, and I want to spend every moment I have left on this planet with you."

She stares at me as if I'm some kind of alien. "Declan?"

"Marry me, Zoe. I don't care where as long as it's as soon as possible. I want you to be my wife, and I want to give you more babies."

Her eyes widen.

"After Daisy actually sleeps through the night." I grin.

"Yes."

"Really?"

She nods, a smile spreading across her lips. "I want to marry you, Declan O'Leary. I want to have more babies. After Daisy sleeps through the night."

I kiss her. I can't help it. This beautiful woman just said yes to marrying me, and all is right with the world.

"Besides ..." She licks her lips. "Third time lucky?"

I roll my eyes. "Shhhh."

And then I kiss her again.

TWENTY-EIGHT
DECLAN

AFTER MY DIVORCE FROM ANNABELLE, if anyone had asked me if I'd ever be married again, I'd have said no.

I would have done Zoe the elaborate wedding of her dreams, but in the end she just wanted a simple ceremony with her parents, Caitlin and Brandon, and our village of people. So that's what I gave her.

We waited until Zoe was ready. I would have married her at her parents' place in Taupo if she'd been ready, but she wanted to marry in the backyard of our home.

And it is a home now.

It's still ridiculously big, but the warmth that she's brought to my life shines through in the décor and the atmosphere. I told her to go crazy redecorating, and while there's still a lot to do, it's a place our family will call home for years and years to come.

I stand at the floral archway in my backyard with Josh Carter at my side as my best man. While I turned my back on acting, I owe him so much for giving me a chance when others wouldn't. The movie we did together was one of the biggest hits of the year, and Nikki fielded all kinds of offers afterward.

To her annoyance, I turned down every single one.

But I have no regrets.

Zoe's contracting. She's doing the programming work she wants to do when she wants to do it. She sets her own hours and she takes a break whenever she wants family time.

And me? I spend every day with my daughter, watching her as she grows, and revelling in being a father.

I never thought this was how my life would turn out. All because I wanted to blow off steam as my career was ending.

Checking my cufflinks for what seems like the thousandth time, I'm a bundle of nerves. Zoe's my dream, but until I see her at the end of that aisle, I'll worry about her changing her mind.

I catch my breath when Zoe appears.

Her mother's sitting nearby with Daisy in her arms. Her father's walking arm-in-arm with Zoe who's dressed in a short, cream lacy wedding gown. She didn't want anything fussy, and Pania begged Zoe to let her design it.

And she's staggeringly beautiful.

I want to drop to my knees and worship my woman, but that can wait until tonight. Tonight, when I have a surprise for her.

Her eyes meet mine as she walks toward me, and she smiles. I'm sure I have stars in my eyes as I watch her. When she joins me, I link our fingers and give her hand a squeeze.

She draws in a deep breath, but the love in her eyes settles any nerves I have.

It's not a long ceremony, but when it comes time for me to recite my vows, I'm so ready.

"Zoe. You turned my whole world upside down. I never thought I'd ever love anyone the way I love you. You're my whole heart. And you've given me the greatest gift I could ever wish for in our daughter. I swear to you today that I'll always love and cherish you. I'll never take what we have for granted, and I'll never get lost again."

Tears fill her eyes. "I love you," she whispers.

"I love you too."

Once the rings are exchanged, and the celebrant declares us husband and wife, I pull her into my arms and kiss her senseless. Our small crowd cheers, and when I pull away, her eyes are glistening with happiness.

I always want her to be this happy.

WE HAVE a luncheon for our reception. My plan is to whisk my bride off for our night away before it gets too late in the evening.

Delaney and Pania cater the food for our small group, and I think I even get brownie points from Brian for the meal they provide.

We're in the dining room, and the women have all deserted the table for the living room. The sound of laughter floats in the air, and happiness settles over me at how well the day has gone.

Brian sits back, content and full, patting his stomach and smiling. "You're doing good, O'Leary. Keep it up."

I grin. "I'm glad to hear it."

"I had my doubts—you know I did, but you've been nothing but good to Zoe. It's a little weird given our ages, but I'm proud to call you my son-in-law."

"Thank you. That means a lot."

He narrows his gaze. "Now, are you going to tell me where you're taking my daughter tonight? She tells me it's a secret."

I chuckle. "It's a surprise for her. But I'll have her back tomorrow as planned, and she can tell you all about it."

His brows rise. "Okay. I'll let you keep your secret."

"She'll be blown away by it. I promise."

Serena enters the room and places a hand on my shoulder. I look up and smile at her. "Good day?"

She nods. "It was beautiful. I'm so glad we're here."

"Couldn't do it without you two. Especially tonight."

Brian wraps his arm around his wife when she sits next to him. "Declan won't tell me where he's taking Zoe later."

Serena rolls her eyes. "It's their wedding. Besides, we get to spend the night with Daisy. I'm looking forward to it."

"It'll be good," I say. "I know Zoe's a little nervous as it's our first whole night without her, but I'll keep her distracted."

Brian shoots me the side-eye. "I do *not* want to know."

Serena and I laugh. It feels good to have family.

By mid-afternoon, I'm done. I want to drag my wife out of there and have my way with her. There's some travel time ahead of us, though, so I have to be patient.

"It's time for us to go," I murmur in her ear, my hands on her waist.

"Oh. I need to see Daisy before we leave."

"I know. I'm not a total monster. Even though I want to get my wife alone as soon as possible."

Zoe's face lights up. "Your wife."

"Yes. You, wife. Me, husband."

Her eyes flash with laughter. "That's going to take some getting used to."

"I know. And now I really want to get to where we're going so I can fuck my wife. So say your goodbyes and let's get out of here."

She turns and cups my cheek with her palm. "You're so cute when you're bossy."

"You'd best get moving then, Mrs O'Leary."

Zoe grins. "I like the sound of that."

I swat her butt. "Go on."

She kisses me hard, and then does the rounds, thanking Delaney and Pania for the food and the dress and for coming, and giving Daisy a cuddle and a kiss before saying goodbye to her parents.

And then finally, we're waving as we head toward the car that's waiting to take us to the airport.

Zoe wanted to organise the wedding—I took care of the wedding night. For all she knows, we're going to a nearby hotel to fuck all night while we make the most of her parents having Daisy.

But I've kept our real destination a secret.

When the car takes the turnoff to LAX, Zoe gasps.

"We're going to the airport? I thought we were heading somewhere close." Her eyes are wild.

"Take a breath, babe. Your parents have Daisy and a ton of expressed milk. I packed your breast pump. Our flight is just over an hour and we're only going overnight. Trust me?" I take her hand in mine.

Her brows are knitted, but she nods.

When we arrive at the airport, we're escorted onto the private jet I've booked.

"Our destination is a surprise." I shoot her a wink, and her eyebrows rise. "But I promise you'll love it."

She leans back in her seat and looks around our surroundings. "I've never been on a private plane before."

Leaning over, I place a gentle kiss on her lips. "That's what I love about you."

"What?" She gives me a confused smile.

"You're so down to earth. You did that insanely huge deal for your app, but flying on a private plane is the last thing from your mind. You're just you."

Her brows twitch. "I'm not sure how to take that."

"Being with you? It's everything. I got so carried away with the lifestyle in the past, but I love nothing more than just being at home with you and Daisy now. You give me a sense of belonging."

Her lower lip wobbles, and she cups my cheek. "Of course you belong."

I kiss her palm. "My whole life, I've never felt this way. You're my home."

"Declan," she whispers.

"So let me treat you like the queen you are tonight."

I kiss her softly and she smiles. "Okay."

She closes her eyes during take-off, and I'm only sad the trip isn't longer to make full use of the bedroom onboard. But we'll be arriving at our destination in an hour, and I want to take my time worshipping my woman's body. We have all night.

It is weird leaving Daisy behind. We might have had evenings out, but this is the first time we've been away from her for a whole night. I just have to do my best to distract Zoe.

And I have so many plans for that.

It's also the first night I've been alone with Zoe in months.

My wife.

It's weird, but though I've been married twice before, the title feels like it should be uniquely Zoe's. I was too young to get married the first time—too drunk to get married the second.

This time, my head is clean and sober, and I'm mature enough to know I'm doing the right thing.

Zoe's my end game.

The bright Las Vegas lights give our location away as we approach, and I smile to myself as her eyes widen and she claps.

"Oh, Declan. This is amazing."

"Wait until you see what else I have in store."

After we're off the plane, I lead her to the limo waiting for us. Our luggage is placed in the back, and I snuggle in the car with my wife.

She squeals when the car pulls up into the familiar circular drive.

"The Bellagio?"

I wrap my arm around her waist and pull her close. "Returning to the scene of the crime."

Zoe laughs. "This is insane."

"This is where you changed my life."

She looks at me with tear-filled eyes. "And you changed mine."

"I remember you telling me the morning after to give you something to remember me by. I'm pretty sure you meant an orgasm, but instead ..."

She buries her face in my neck as we pull up outside.

"Let's get out of the car. The porter will take the bags up. I even managed to book the same suite."

"No way."

I step out of the door and hold my hand out to help Zoe from the car. Her whole face is lit up with excitement.

When we've checked in, we make our way to the elevator and up to the suite. I swipe the card to open the door and then push it open. I dip and sweep Zoe into my arms as she laughs.

"What are you doing?" she asks.

"Everything properly." I grin, carrying her through the door and kicking it closed.

After carrying her all the way to the bed, I gently lower her down and kiss her like my life depends on it. I love this woman with all my heart—I never, ever want another.

Our love story started here and it will continue tonight.

"This is where we make memories—new ones. I know our first time here is hazy for you because of the champagne, but I remember every moment. If I'd realised—"

She grasps my arms. "You had just as much to drink as I did. I remember enough."

"What do you remember?"

Zoe bites her bottom lip "How talented you were with your tongue?"

I pull my tie off and drop it on the floor. "Glad I impressed you."

"Maybe you should get over here, and I'll show you how impressive I can be with *my* tongue."

"Why don't you do just that, Mrs O'Leary?"

She reaches for my belt. Her fingers make light work of the buckle, and she slides it through the loops on my pants and throws it to the ground.

"The one thing that annoyed me about our first night together was that my memory doesn't match yours for the first night we spent together. You might remember my lips wrapped around your cock, but I don't." As if to stretch out the anticipation, she runs her tongue across her red-painted lips.

She fiddles with the button on my slacks, undoes it and slides the zip down.

I'm hard as a rock by the time she releases my cock from my boxers.

I let out a moan as she slides her warm, hot mouth along my length. Closing my eyes, I let my wife do whatever she wants with me, her tongue flicking up and down the side of my cock, and I jolt as she licks my tip.

She sets up a rhythm. I want so badly to be buried inside her pussy, but she grasps my balls and rolls them gently in her hand, and I lose control.

I run my fingers through her hair. She fixes her gaze on mine, and I'm a goner. My body tenses, my balls tighten, and I come down her throat. Zoe stays there, her hand around my cock, her mouth around the tip until she gets every last drop before she sits up and licks her lips. Her hair is mussed, but it's the satisfied grin on her face that gets me.

Everything's sweeter the second time around.

TWENTY-NINE
ZOE

Two years later

BUTTERFLIES ARE BREEDING in my stomach.

It's the only rational explanation as to why I feel like something's taken flight in my abdomen—although it could also be the baby growing inside me.

Once again, I'm on the red carpet and five months' pregnant.

I smooth my dress down and take a deep breath.

Declan's presenting an award at the Oscars tonight—Best Adapted Screenplay for which Jessie and her co-writer, Adam Walton, have been nominated. They adapted Jessie's life story for a movie about her past—*Interrupted Life*.

Never did I think I'd be going to the Oscars, let alone walking the red carpet. But it's all happening tonight.

Declan walks into the room, adjusting his cufflinks as he goes. He's such an effortlessly handsome man, but in a tux? Turns up the hot factor by a million. "You look beautiful."

"So do you."

He grins. Life has been a fairy tale since we moved in together. And for tonight, Pania designed my dress, and for only the second time in my life I've had professional hair and makeup people pampering me in my own home.

I've never felt better.

He pulls me into his arms. "Can I kiss you, or will it upset the makeup?"

"You'd better kiss me."

He laughs, and plants one on me. "I love you, Zoe. I'm looking forward to taking my girl out."

My parents are here for a visit. Declan and I have had dates with Delaney or Lana babysitting, but I know Daisy is in good hands tonight with my mother. Dad and Declan still circle each other from time to time, and the testosterone gets a bit too much, but they both love and want to protect me—one day they'll work it out.

Delaney waves at us as we walk the red carpet, and I wave back before we join her. Josh is off posing for photos.

"This is Zoe's first Oscar ceremony." Declan places a kiss on my temple, and I sigh a little as he waves and then walks toward Josh.

"I remember my first. I was terrified." Delaney sighs. "It's all a bit overwhelming."

"Can I ask you something?"

Delaney nods. "Sure."

"Does this ever go away? That sick feeling in your stomach over all this attention?"

She shakes her head. "It's the part of Josh's life I like the least. But I do it because I'm proud of him, and I want to send a message to the world that he belongs to me."

I grin. "I didn't think of that."

"You'll be fine. Just stick with us." Delaney clasps my hand in hers and tucks me against her side.

"I guess you're an old hand at this."

She smiles. "I hate it, but I'm here for Josh. That's what I keep telling myself. Besides, Pania, Lana, and Jessie aren't far behind us, and we're definitely partying after this is done with. If you'd like to join us ...?"

I shift my gaze to Declan, catching his eye. He winks and nods at me. "We'd love to."

"He's so gorgeous," Delaney says.

"I know." I laugh. "Josh is pretty nice eye candy too."

Her smile lights up her whole face. "He really is. I think we're both very lucky women."

"Who's lucky? Pania's lucky." Reece's drawl comes from behind us.

I turn and see Reece and Pania approaching. My stomach flips. All these movie stars in one place is a bit much—even if we're all friends now.

"Oh please, you're the lucky one." Pania rolls her eyes.

"I know I am." He pulls her into his arms and nuzzles her neck.

"Zoe's the lucky one. We've all seen that sex tape." Pania shrugs.

"Pania," Delaney snaps.

"Sorry." She bites her bottom lip.

I shrug. "I'm not. I've seen it too."

We all laugh, and that tight feeling in my chest eases a little. I'm safe, I'm with friends, and I'm with the love of my life.

Delaney lets go of my hand as Josh approaches, smiling when he wraps an arm around her waist.

Declan captures my hand and raises it to his lips. And then I'm lost in his eyes, his confidence washing over me.

"Have I told you how beautiful you look tonight?" he murmurs.

"Declan ..."

"I'm so in love with you, Zoe. I know you feel like a fish out of water right now, but your place is by my side. You know that, right?"

I shrug. "You're here with all these glamorous women and I—"

"You are the only one I see. Besides, this is the last time I'll do one of these award shows."

I blink rapidly. He might not be acting anymore, but I never thought for a moment that he was finished with the whole lifestyle. "What?"

"It might have been me twenty years ago, but I'd much rather be at home cuddled up with you and our girl. If you want to dress up and come out to these things, then I'll be with you, but this just isn't me anymore."

Huffing out a breath, I stand there like a fish, my mouth gaping open.

"Declan, I can't ask you to give this up," I whisper.

"I'm not giving up anything I don't want to. I'll give you

nights out, but we never have to do this red carpet bullshit again."

"Oh thank God."

He chuckles as I fall into his arms and he kisses the top of my head. "I love you, Zoe. You're all I need."

Linking our fingers together, he leads me to our seats. We're sitting not far from Josh and Delaney with Jessie and her husband Shane on the other side.

When the ceremony starts, I barely know where to look. I've never seen so many Hollywood stars, and it's a very different experience to watching the Oscars on TV. I laugh, and I cry, and when Declan has to go backstage to get ready to present, I smile at the seat filler who takes his place.

Those nervous butterflies start up again.

And then his name's announced and when he appears, my heart swells with pride. I've watched these shows for years, but never thought I'd be in the crowd.

And right up there on that stage is the man I love—the father of my child.

He smiles. "Adapting a screenplay from an existing story is a labour of love. Frequently, filmmakers become infatuated with a story, and when that happens, it's magic."

"The nominees for Best Adapted Screenplay are ..."

I turn my head to watch Jessie. She takes a big breath, and Shane reaches for her hand and gives her a loving smile. Crossing my fingers, I shift my gaze back to Declan.

When he opens the envelope, his grin is a mile wide, and my stomach flips in anticipation. "And the Oscar goes to Jessie Lane and Adam Walton for *Interrupted Life*."

Everyone around me erupts into applause. Then we're all

on our feet as Jessie hugs Shane tight before making her way to the stage where Declan kisses her cheek and gives her the award.

It takes a moment before the clapping stops, and Jessie wipes a tear from her cheek.

"Thank you," she croaks. "I'll make this quick."

Taking a deep breath, she continues. "This has been such a hard journey that started when I was fifteen years old, and I can only hope that my story helps put a stop to abuse in our industry. I want to thank Adam Walton, who's at home with the flu tonight, for helping me translate my story into the screenplay that gave it justice. And most of all, I want to thank my husband, Shane, for loving me unconditionally and giving me the strength to come forward." She holds up the award. "I dedicate this to anyone who's ever been hurt by the Hollywood casting couch or variations thereof. Thank you."

She leaves the stage to rapturous applause. It wasn't that long ago that speaking up about abuse would never have happened. I admire her strength and her honesty about everything she went through.

When Declan rejoins me, I grasp his arm. He kisses my temple, and I sigh contentedly.

Do I want to do this again? Not really.

Would I be happier curled up on the couch with Declan? Definitely.

But right now I'm just happy to be with him to celebrate our friend's success.

Life couldn't be sweeter.

EPILOGUE
ZOE

Three years later

MY BEAUTIFUL HUSBAND IS FIFTY. The grey's encroaching into his dark hair even farther, but he's as gorgeous as he's ever been.

And utterly dedicated to his family.

I thought he'd cave when the offers flooded in when his movie was released, but he turned his back on Hollywood in every way.

Except one.

Now he mentors young actors who find fame at an early age, and he teaches them what not to do. He and Jessie formed a foundation to help people abused by the system or who need guidance in difficult situations. It's growing every year as more celebrities want to be a part of it to try to stop the sins of the past from carrying into the future.

The work is rewarding, but for Declan, nothing beats being a father.

Pushing myself back from my desk, I stand and walk into the kitchen. A loud squeal makes me look toward the corner of the garden where my husband sits at a table, making pretend tea with our girls.

A little over two years after Daisy, we welcomed Delilah to our little family.

Declan's never shown any signs of returning to his old life—he relishes the new one too much to ever put it at risk. He's such a doting dad, he puts me to shame. I don't have the patience to sit and pour imaginary cups of tea from a plastic teapot. But Declan will be there until the girls get sick of it and want to move onto something else.

"I want to go on the swing. Push me, Daddy," Daisy cries.

"Me too." Delilah joins in.

Tea party abandoned, they run toward the swing set nearby. Declan helps them both into the swings and gives them a gentle push.

I shake my head and head back inside to my desk. They'll be entertained by him for long enough for me to get some work done before dinner.

When the squealing stops, Delilah comes running in and heads straight toward me. I turn and open my arms as she leaps on my lap.

"Nap time," she tells me.

"Is it?" I kiss her cheek. "Have you had fun with Daddy?"

"Swings."

"I know, sweetie."

"Del, come on. How about you and your sister come upstairs with me?" Declan shoots me a wink as he leads Daisy and then Delilah upstairs. Daisy's growing out of her naps, but she follows her younger sister upstairs regardless. They'll be out for at least a couple of hours once Declan works his magic.

I'm lost in thought when footsteps fall behind me.

He nuzzles my neck. "What are you up to?"

"I'm working on something new. Want to see?"

Declan grins. We called time on our family once our second daughter was born. Declan didn't want to be an older father, and my second pregnancy was plagued with complications. Nothing serious ended up being wrong, but there were enough complications that I didn't want to do it again.

Our life together is perfect.

But I turned out to be the one with itchy feet, and while I know I never have to work again, I couldn't stay away.

"I'm making a new chat platform. I saw something online about a gaming company wanting to create a safe platform for the gamers to chat on. They're widening their range of games to include a younger target market, and they have a system, but it's pretty open. So, I got in touch with the CEO, and she loved my ideas. I'm building a trial system, but something that can scale if they opt to buy it."

His eyebrows rise. "So, you're working for free?"

I shake my head. "No way. Apparently some of her employees used my dating app and raved about it, so she knows my work history. Plus, doing it in-house means either employing new developers or reassigning people to do this, so I'm contracting to her for the moment."

"What does 'for the moment' mean? Are you going to work for her?"

I cup his face in my hands. God, how I love this man. He's always looking out for me.

"No. It's just a contract. If this works the way I think it will, then I can work up a maintenance plan and hand it off to them. If they run into any issues or want more features, then I'll come in again on short term contracts." I plant a kiss on his lips. "It works for both of us, and it means I'm not committed to working full-time."

"I'm so proud of you." He runs his fingers through my hair. "But the girls are napping, so ..."

"So, it's time for me to step away from the computer."

He grins. "Something like that."

We walk upstairs together. Once we established ourselves in LA, surrounded by our village, we never looked back. I sold my apartment in San Francisco, and we turned Declan's crazy house into a home with the girls.

Caitlin sometimes travels with Brandon now—especially when they come to LA to play, and their two boys are as close to my girls as they can be. He's now talking retirement, and they want to settle nearby.

We've all landed on our feet.

The girls will be asleep for a couple of hours, so Declan and I take our time undressing and slipping into bed. I live for these lazy afternoons with Declan. While there are times when we rip each other's clothes off, hungry for one another, there are also these times where things are slow and gentle.

He places his weight over me, and I grasp his biceps. I love this moment where I feel my husband's strength under my fingers. When he kisses me, I get lost in the sensation. His kisses are as amazing as they were from day one, and I sigh a little as he drops his lips to my neck before working his way down my body. My man's still a big fan of oral sex.

And when he slides into me, I sigh again contentedly, rising to meet every thrust until he's the one who calls *my* name.

Afterward, I rest my head on his chest, which now features all our names tattooed near his heart.

"I never thought I'd be this happy. For years I thought I had to be someone to find that fulfilment from life when what I really needed was you and our girls," he says.

I place a kiss on his chest. "You *are* someone. You're the love of my life, and you're the whole world to those girls."

His dark eyes drink me in. "Love of your life, huh?"

"I don't know any other way to describe you." I smile. "All I know is that I plan on spending the rest of my time on earth with you."

"Feeling's mutual, babe," he murmurs. "This. Us. The kids. I feel like I was floating for years with nowhere to land, but you brought me back to solid ground."

Tears well in my eyes. "I'm so glad we found each other."

"Me too."

"Mamma," a little voice calls from a nearby room.

I chuckle. "Time's up, Mr O'Leary."

He sighs. "I knew getting this much quiet time was a lot to ask for."

"We still have tonight."

"And every night." He kisses me on the nose.

"I love you, Declan."

And I always will.

ALSO BY WENDY SMITH

Coming Home

Doctor's Orders

Baker's Dozen

Hunter's Mark

Teacher's Pet

A Very Campbell Christmas

Fall and Rise Duet

Falling

Rising

Fall and Rise - The Complete Duet

The Aeon Series

Game On

Build a Nerd

Bar None

Hollywood Kiwis Series

Common Ground

Even Ground

Under Ground

Rocky Ground

Solid Ground

Stand alones

For the Love of Chloe

Only Ever You

The Friends Duet

Loving Rowan

Three Days

The Forever Series

Something Real

The Right One

Unexpected

Chances Series

Another Chance

Taking Chances

Lifetime Series

In a Lifetime

In an Instant

In a Heartbeat

In the End

At the Start

ABOUT THE AUTHOR

Wendy Smith lives with her two children and two cats in Hastings, New Zealand, and she's not sure who's responsible for her grey hair. She's a multi-platform bestselling author, whose book In the End, written as Ariadne Wayne, was named one of Apple's best books of 2017. All her stories come with a quirky sense of humour, and she cries over everything.

Find me online
www.wendysmith.co.nz
wendy@wendysmith.co.nz